THE LONELY SHADOWS AND OTHER STORIES

The midnight moon rode high and the house seemed to transmute the moonlight into something terrible. The broken chimneys stretched up like hands to the heavens, the eyeless sockets of the windows staring intently along the twisting drive. On the floor of the library, strange cabalistic designs glowed with an eerie light and there was a flickering as of corpse candles — a cold radiance, a manifestation of the evil aura which had never left this place, instead crystallising inside its very walls . . .

JOHN GLASBY

THE LONELY SHADOWS

AND OTHER STORIES

Complete and Unabridged

LINFORD
Leicester

First published in Great Britain

First Linford Edition
published 2013

A catalogue record for this book is available
from the British Library.

ISBN 978–1–4448–1689–1

Published by
F. A. Thorpe (Publishing)
Anstey, Leicestershire

Set by Words & Graphics Ltd.
Anstey, Leicestershire
Printed and bound in Great Britain by
T.J. International Ltd., Padstow, Cornwall

This book is printed on acid-free paper

For Edmund

1

The Lonely Shadows

The house stood well back from the road, only partly hidden by the bare arms of the leafless trees, thrust up against the scudding clouds; gaunt, gnarled branches which rattled eerily in the chill wind. Its lines were still good in spite of its age, tall and elegant in places; and there was still an air of importance and pride in the paintless fluted columns on either side of the door. Three tall chimneys hugged the gables on one side, but all were chipped and ragged about the edges and in one of them, birds had built their nest some years before. Dilapidated and unmistakably old, it stood, or rather seemed to hunch itself forward in an attitude of waiting beyond the unkempt lawns and straggling bushes which lined the gravel, weed-covered drive.

Jeremiah Calder stood for a long

moment with his right hand on the gate, wondering for an instant — as he always did whenever he came here — why he felt so strangely hesitant about going in. Even from the roadway, from where he stood, it was possible to *feel* the air of desolation about this particular house. Or was it just desolation? There seemed an air of malignant waiting about the place now, which he had never noticed or felt before. He became conscious of the watchfulness of the house, acutely aware of the shuttered windows on the lower floor, green paint flaking from the wood, and the upstairs windows, open like eyes in a skull, staring sightlessly along the drive in his direction. Watching and considering what he intended to do now, he thought inwardly, then pulled himself together angrily, shrugging his shoulders quickly and pulling up the collar of his heavy coat around his neck.

God! He thought angrily, he was getting to be almost as jumpy and as imaginative as that foolish young clerk of his. He had known better than to send him down here on this particular occasion, having decided that it was essential he should come himself. This was quite clearly a matter that would have to be handled with the utmost tact and diplomacy.

Gripping the handle of his briefcase tightly he walked as quickly along the drive as his sixty-three years would allow and hammered on the front door, the heavy brass knocker sending hollow echoes chasing themselves through the house. He smiled wryly to himself, remembering the day when he had first visited Belstead House. Even though that had been more than forty years ago, he could recall it as clearly as if it had been the previous summer.

It had been a hot July afternoon with the sky a cloudless mirror of blue-white, the sun throwing few shadows and the shimmering heat lying in a thick blanket over everything. That had been the day when Charles Henry Belstead arrived from London to claim his inheritance, the house and the grounds, which he had been left by his austere-faced father and quite a sizeable fortune to go with it. Old

Mr. Peters, his predecessor, dead these twenty-seven years, had been the family solicitor in those days and he had been a very junior clerk in the office.

As he had been shown into the house on that hot summer day, he had felt self-conscious, the centre of attraction and a little unsure of what was expected of him; and the sight of the polished coffin at the back of the room had almost completely unnerved him from the start of the proceedings. Somehow, he had managed to get through the reading of the will and all other necessary details without making himself appear unduly foolish but all the time, every single second, he had been acutely aware of the long, polished box with the shining brass handles immediately at his back, had almost seemed to feel eyes boring malignantly into his skull.

It had all been his imagination, of course, nothing more and once out of the house he had soon got over it. But there was one thing he had never been able to get out of his mind, something concerning Charles Belstead. Before his arrival at

4

Belstead House, it had been doubtful if he had visited the place, or his father, half a dozen times in twice as many years. From what Calder had heard, the other had been leading a rather riotous life in London. When his father had died, leaving him one of the richest men in that part of the country, everyone had expected him to sell the old house and go back to London, to pick up the threads of his old way of living again. But to the immense surprise of everyone in the village, he had simply shut himself up in the house and remained there as a recluse all these years. Not once had he left the grounds, and indeed, he had seldom been seen outside the house itself.

There had been an old housekeeper, the only one of the servants to remain after his father had died, but she too, had died almost seven years before and since her death, Charles Belstead had lived entirely alone, shunned by those around him. He neither sought, nor wanted friends.

Calder's thoughts snapped back to the present and he hammered on the door with the knocker again. Once more, echoes rumbled mournfully through the house, but this time, he heard the shuffling footsteps coming closer and a moment later, the door creaked open.

Overhead, a cloud-veil crept across the face of the moon and darkness seemed to crouch like a living thing around the house.

'Yes, who is it?' The thin, reedy voice sent a faint shiver along Calder's spine. He pushed himself forward a few inches, saw the narrow, pinched face that stared out at him through the crack in the doorway.

'Jeremiah Calder,' he said quietly. 'You asked me to call and see you. In fact you were most insistent that I should come tonight.'

'Ah yes, so I did.' The other seemed to have difficulty in remembering, but he opened the door further and stood on one side as Calder went inside. A draft of cold air swirled briefly about him and the little shiver came back from his body as he realised that the coldness had come from inside the house, not from outside. He glanced about him, noticing that nothing had changed since that day when he had first entered this house. Dust lay everywhere. The thick, heavy drapes on the walls were ragged and frayed at the edges. From the walls themselves, their faces in the long, gilt-framed pictures, stared down through a thickness of paint that had faded appreciably over the years. The feel of death was here, growing stronger every time he came.

'If this is something important,' he said slowly, keeping his voice calm and even, though with an effort, 'it would really have been best for us to have talked at my office. There are a lot of details that — '

'We'll have no argument,' snapped the other quickly. 'We'll talk in the library. If you'll just go along, I'll join you in a minute. You know the way.'

Rebuffed, Calder watched the other hobble into one of the rooms and close the door behind him. Shrugging his shoulders, he made his way along the wide corridor, which led almost the whole of the way through the house, into the library at the back. A sudden, brief flash of lightning lit the window set in one wall and a few moments later, there was a fierce rumble of thunder in the near distance, shaking the heavens. He was going to get wet walking back to the village, he reflected wearily. Sighing, he twisted the handle of the library door and went inside. There were candles burning on the piano set on a raised portion of the floor, in front of the wide, French windows and the small fire burning in the hearth.

For a moment, he waited in motionless silence, feeling that something was about to happen, but not knowing, or even able to guess, what it might be. There came a brilliant flash of lightning which illuminated the garden outside the French windows, showed up for one brief moment the dripping arms of the tree which swayed just outside, the bushes whipped to a sudden frenzy at the strong wind that had sprung up. Then a sudden movement caught his eye, attracted his attention from the scene outside.

There was a second door in the library, leading out towards the kitchens at the eastern side of the old house. It had been tightly closed when he had first walked into the room. Now, it was open and he saw the tall figure that stood there, looking in at him with an expression of curiosity on the shadowed face. He started forward, a little hesitant. Belstead had not mentioned that there was anyone else staying at the house with him and he felt surprise more than any other emotion.

Even as he went forward, the other backed away into the passage where the shadows were thick and huge.

'Don't go,' said Jeremiah Calder quickly. 'I'm sorry if I startled you, but I — ' He reached the door and jerked it wide, going out into the corridor. There was a single candle placed on a table at the far end of the passage throwing long, flickering shadows along the walls. But the passage itself was empty and he knew that it would have been impossible for the other to have moved so quickly along it, certainly without making a sound. Puzzled, he went back into the room. There had been something oddly familiar about the face he had seen, but he was unable to place it. His memory was not quite as good as it used to be, he reflected inwardly. Perhaps he had imagined it all, but somehow, he didn't think so. That face which had peered into the room at him — there seemed to be something malignant about it. Almost as if the other had known that he was there — alone.

Belstead came into the room a moment later. He motioned Jeremiah to a chair, then lowered himself into the other. He seemed even older than Calder remembered him from the last time they had met, less than two months before. His eyes were sunk deep into his head and even as Calder watched, he noticed that they kept flicking from one corner of the room to the other, then across to the windows that opened out on to the lawn.

Belstead had brought in a bottle of wine and two glasses that he had set on the small table between them. Even the top of the table, Calder noticed, was covered with a thin film of grey dust and there were strands of cobweb on the neck of the bottle. He sipped the red wine slowly, then nodded appreciatively.

'Good,' he said quietly. 'But that was one thing about your father, Charles. He always kept an excellent cellar here.'

'He kept a lot of other things besides,' said the other in a strange voice. He sat hunched forward in the chair, eyes moving continually. He lifted his head slightly and shot Calder a sharp glance. 'You think that it's strange I should have stayed here all of these years, don't you? Oh, it's no use lying to me, Jeremiah, we have known each other too long for that. I know too, what the people in the village say about me. A lot of inquisitive busybodies, nothing else. They think I'm insane to stay here when I could have been out enjoying myself, with a world cruise every year, house in London.'

'Then why don't you leave? Surely there's nothing to stop you now. You're living here all alone, especially after your housekeeper died. Is there any reason why you should have to remain here?' Calder eyed the other narrowly over the rim of his glass. Inwardly, he tried to recall if there had been anything in the old man's will when he had left everything to his son, forbidding him to leave the house. But he could remember nothing. It was almost, he reflected idly, as though the other were afraid to go out. A man who shunned the sunlight and lived here, shut away from the outside world, all alone.

Or was he quite alone? That man he had seen looking in at him through the other door — why was it that even the memory of that face, which he had glimpsed only for a brief fraction of a second, sent a little shiver coursing up and down his spine. Certainly there had been nothing malevolent about the figure he had seen — except for the fact that the other seemed to have vanished into thin air, although the probable explanation of that was that he had disappeared into one of the other rooms along the wide corridor. Possibly some friend of Belstead's who had come upon him suddenly, realised his mistake, and left equally unobtrusively. Still, the thought bothered him more than he cared to admit. He grew aware that the other was speaking slowly, but with an odd intensity in his quavering voice.

'Tell me, Jeremiah. As a lawyer and a friend, do you believe that the dead can come back?'

For a moment, Calder sat upright in his chair, shocked, stunned almost by the other's question. Perhaps he ought to have expected something like this, he thought quickly, but it had been put so bluntly that for a moment, it had taken him completely by surprise.

'I'm afraid I'm not sure how to answer that question, Charles.' He forced a quick, slightly strained, smile. 'To be quite legal, I'd like notice of it.'

'I'm not joking. This is perfectly serious.' He laughed a little shrilly, and his eyes were never still, as though he expected to see something leaping for him out of the shadows around the wide hearth. 'I know what you're thinking. No use in denying it, I can see it written all over your face. You never were very good at hiding your feelings, especially from me. You're thinking that the solitude here has made me a little mad. But you're wrong, quite wrong. Actually, what it has done is to make me see things a little more clearly than I ever did before.'

Calder set down his empty glass, hesitated. There came nine mournful, dismal chimes from the clock in the hallway outside. Deep, sepulchral tones which chased each other along the hollow, empty corridor.

'Do I shock you?' went on the other harshly. He leaned back in his chair, the firelight throwing the shrunken flesh of his scrawny neck into shadow. He looked old and wizened, thought Calder tightly, like a man who had slowly, but surely been sucked dry of all the juices, all the strength, that had once been his, in those days before he had come here.

'A little, Charles,' he admitted. A log crackled sharply in the hearth, threw a shower of spitting, red sparks up the chimney. Outside, the storm seemed to have increased in intensity and thunder rumbled and toned like a maddened beast over the house. Calder rose slowly to his feet and stood to one side of the hearth, his hands clasped tightly behind him, keeping a tight grip on himself. He had to get to the bottom of this, he knew that with a sudden certainty. The other had called him here, on a night like this, and at short notice, so that there had to be something in what he said. If not, then it might be best if he were to humour him; at least until he got back to the village and had a confidential chat with Doctor Woodbridge. If there was anything wrong with the other's mind, it was essential that the doctor should know about it as soon as possible. Perhaps the shock of his housekeeper's death had affected Belstead a little more than they had realised at the time.

'I thought I might.' The other sucked in his thin lips, sipped his drink slowly, occasionally pausing to glance, bird-like, up at the lawyer. Pointedly, he said: 'I asked you to come ahead into the library for a purpose. You possibly know what it was by now.' The bright eyes never left Calder's face for a single instant.

'I'm afraid that I don't.'

'No? That's odd. When I came in here, you looked as though you'd seen a ghost. You hadn't, had you?'

'Of course not.' Calder felt a little wave of anger wash through him. He bit down the biting retort that threatened to spring to his lips and went on calmly. 'It isn't right that you should stay here any longer, Charles. I've been worried about you on and off for the past two years. You aren't getting any younger, you know and there's no telling what might happen to you if you persist staying here alone. And you've got to remember that it's the best part of three miles to the nearest house if you should need help of any kind, and you don't have a telephone here.'

'Why should I need help from anyone?' demanded the other harshly. He put down his glass, paused for a moment then poured himself another drink, moving the bottle towards Calder's glass, pouring another as the lawyer nodded. 'But coming back to the other point I made. You did see someone — or something — when you came in here first, didn't you?' His eyes were dark and unwinking as they bored into the other's. 'You're no longer quite as sure of yourself as you were. I can see that from your face.'

Calder sat down again in his chair, gulped down his drink quickly, felt some of the warmth come back into his body, driving out the nameless chill which had settled over him like a shroud. He took out a cigarette, one of the few luxuries in which he allowed himself to indulge, and lit it with fingers that trembled a little, even though he tried his hardest to keep them still.

Blowing smoke into the air, he sat back, then finished his drink completely before saying: 'How long have you lived here by yourself, Charles? Forty years isn't it, almost exactly to the day. As I recall, it was mid-summer when you first came, and virtually every one of the servants had left by the following December. I wonder why they did leave like that.' He eyed the other obliquely. 'Could it have been because of that temper of yours — or was there some other reason?'

'You're still intent on trying to prove that I'm insane, aren't you?' The thin, bloodless lips were pursed into a tight line. 'I'm not sure why you're doing it.

Either you think that will make things easier for you, or you're getting to be frightened yourself and you're deliberately trying to convince yourself. But you saw something and you're still wondering whether or not it was your imagination.'

'I may have seen something,' admitted the other reluctantly. 'But I'm not prepared to believe that it was anything out of the normal. I must confess that I had thought you were alone in this house. Everyone in the village thought that too. But if you aren't, well that's your affair entirely. Perhaps you'd like to talk about it.' *Better humour the other,* he thought grimly. Evidently there was something on his mind and if he talked about it, it might help him.

Outside, the thunder rolled and roared savagely, beating like some huge fist against the heavens. An occasional flash of lightning lit the grotesque limbs of the trees beyond the windows as the branches swayed and tossed in some weird devil-dance. With an effort, Calder tore his gaze away and concentrated on what Belstead was saying. The other smiled thinly at him, frowning a little.

'The funny thing is that I never really understood why my father hated me so much. It was almost as if he were insanely jealous of everything I did. I left home when I was eighteen, determined I had to get out on my own, otherwise his will would have dominated mine entirely. He was that kind of man. You may remember him too, even though it was over forty years ago.'

'I do recall that he was determined to have his own way in everything he did,' acknowledged Calder quietly. 'But knowing his personality, I hardly think things could have turned out otherwise. He was an extremely strong-willed man. More so than almost anyone I've ever met. But I never knew that he hated you.'

'You think that I'm exaggerating somewhat.' Belstead shook his head. 'I assure you that I'm not. If anything, I'm understating the position. I was the only child. My mother died when I was seven. I don't remember much about her. My only impressions of her are of a tall, pale woman who did her best to fall in with my father's wishes; someone who seemed content to stay in the background, the perfect foil to his own personality. You know, I think that in this world, it can only be the cruel and ruthless people who are ever successful.' He smiled again, weakly. 'Perhaps success is the reward for cruelty, who knows? But he was successful. No matter what he did, no matter what he turned his hand to, it was highly successful. He was a very rich man when he died. I'd been in London for a good many years then, only coming back here to see him when I had to. Oh, I know what the people in the village used to say about me behind my back. There goes an ungrateful son who takes everything his father gives and yet gives nothing in return, who squanders every penny of his allowance, a very generous allowance, and yet comes home to see his father only once in two years.' He broke off and ran a finger down the side of his long nose reflectively. 'I sometimes wonder what those people would have said if they had only known the truth. They saw only the side of him that he wanted them to see.

They didn't often come into contact with him, as I did before I left home. To them, he was the rich and powerful man who donated huge sums of money for hospitals and schools, who gave money prizes to the pupils, helped them with grants. But that was only money that he was giving away, and he had more than enough of that to spare. He never missed any of it. Perhaps he even thought that the more he gave away, the less there would be for me when he finally died.'

'Aren't you being a little harsh in your judgement? After all, it's been more than forty years — '

'You think that's long enough for hate to die?' blazed the other fiercely. 'Real hate, I mean! No, I remember these things only too clearly and as I said before, being here alone in this house for so long has made me see things a lot more clearly than I ever did before.'

'What sort of things?' There was a change in the atmosphere of the room. A change that Calder could feel, but that was extremely hard for him to define.

'I remember coming home once — I

think I must have been almost twenty at the time. I caught an earlier train than I usually did and no one was expecting me when I arrived. I'd walked from the station across the fields, because it was such a beautiful afternoon, coming in over the wall at the back and through the gardens. I came over the lawn and through those windows there — at least, I meant to come in that way — but I didn't.'

'Why on earth not?' Calder felt a strange tightening of the muscles of his chest and he knew that his breathing was a little harsh on the back of his throat. He ought not to be listening to talk such as this, he told himself fiercely. The other had evidently become obsessed by something that had happened all those long years ago, something with probably quite a simple explanation, but his mind had caught hold of it, twisted it, warped it into something far removed from the actual proof, until now he could not get it out of his mind, and it had taken over control of him almost entirely. This was how hate could distort anyone's outlook, if one allowed it to take a tight hold.

Belstead paused for a long moment, then leaned forward holding out his skinny hands to the blaze as though for warmth. There was a curious expression on his wizened features and his eyes seemed brighter than usual, with something lurking in their depths that Calder had never seen before and which made him feel a little afraid.

'I can remember it all so clearly as if it were yesterday and not almost forty-five years ago. I knew there was someone in the library before I reached the windows, because I heard the mutter of voices as I crossed the lawn. But I thought it was just father and the housekeeper having one of their never-ending arguments. She was a domineering woman too and they clashed far too often for my liking. But as I got closer, I realised that it wasn't the housekeeper, although I could hear my father's voice quite plainly. It was a man's voice I heard talking to him, but one that, at the moment, I didn't recognise, although it was familiar. For some reason that I can't explain, I felt scared. That voice was one I had heard before, though why it should have frightened me like that I didn't know as I stood out there on the lawn, behind the bushes, hidden from them, wondering whether or not I ought to cough and make my presence known. You might think that was making a mountain out of a molehill, but I've already explained that my father hated me, he had a really violent temper when he was roused. So I crept forward quite slowly, without making a sound, and peered into the windows. I could see the whole of this room quite clearly. As I said, it was a fine, sunny afternoon, and the sunlight came directly into the library at that time of the day.'

'Go on,' prompted Calder quietly. 'If you want to get this off your chest, it will do you good to talk to me. After all, what is a friend for?' The words were more reassuring than the tone of the voice.

'My father was there, standing in the middle of the room. There were three other people with him, not one as I thought. They were standing around the room, watching him. He was — ' the other broke off a moment as though finding it difficult to continue, then he swallowed jerkily and went on: 'He was standing inside some strange markings that had been drawn on the floor, where the big carpet had been rolled back out of the way.'

'Strange markings?' echoed Calder. 'What sort of markings were they? Do you know?'

'I didn't then. But I do now.' The other spoke with a dark significance. 'He had drawn a circle inside a five-sided figure and there were small metal cups, they looked like silver, at each point of the pentagon. In the sunlight, I could see that there was some kind of clear liquid in them.'

The shiver inside Calder's body grew a little, became more insistent. 'Are you absolutely certain about this?' he asked hoarsely. 'You didn't imagine it all?'

'Imagine it? Jeremiah, you don't imagine things like that. I'd never seen anything like it before and if it had been nothing more than that, it would have stuck in my mind. I assure you.'

'Then there was something more?'
Somehow, Calder got the question out,
although he felt a little sick inside.

'Those three people who were with my
father in the library. I hadn't recognised
the voice at first, but I did recognise the
faces. Doctor Talbot and his wife and
Colonel Carter. They were all fairly
frequent visitors to our house when I was
a small boy but they — '

Calder stared at him incredulously, as
though unable to believe his ears. He
finished the other's sentence for him in a
voice that was not very steady. 'All three
of them had died before you were ten
years old.'

★ ★ ★

An hour later, when the storm had abated
a little, and the thunder was beating at
the distant horizon, with the full moon
striving to break through the scudding
clouds overhead, Jeremiah Calder left the
old house and walked back a little
hurriedly along the overgrown drive
towards the gate. He had tried vainly to

get Belstead to come with him, to put up at one of the two hotels in the village, had even offered to put him up himself, but the other had steadfastly refused to accompany him. There had been something infinitely pathetic about that old man, old in mind and body, sitting there in front of the dying fire in the library — a room that must have held a host of horrible secrets. But he had been determined too. It had been impossible to tell whether or not the other had been afraid. If not, it could only have been because he was now so used to these things, that his mind no longer thought about them. He accepted them as something he had lived with most of his life and which he would have to go on living with until he died. Then perhaps, thought Calder inwardly, the house might really be empty.

He opened the gate, stepped through and latched it behind him. A few heavy drops of rain patted down on him from the dripping branches of the trees, which overlooked the lonely road leading back to the village. A strange little thought popped unbidden into his mind as he paused for a moment and stared back over his shoulder towards the looming bulk of the house. *Was there just the possibility that when Charles Belstead died, the house would be — not empty, but full?*

Back in his room, he made himself some hot coffee, drank it so quickly that it burned his tongue and the back of his throat. After that, he felt a little better. His first thought had been to dismiss entirely what he had heard from Charles Belstead that night. Looking back on it, trying to review everything that the other had said in an objective manner, it made little sense. Most of what he had told him could have stemmed from his strange sense of hatred that appeared to have existed between father and son. But did that explain fully why Charles Belstead had refused to leave the house after he had inherited it?

He checked his watch, saw that it was a little after ten-thirty. Woodbridge might still be up, he thought, and at a moment like this, he felt that he needed some practical medical advice about Belstead.

Woodbridge answered the phone almost immediately, his voice crisp and alert. Evidently he had not yet gone to bed.

'Calder here, Henry,' he said quietly. 'I was wondering if I could have a talk with you — tonight. It's important and I'd like your advice on a problem that has just come up.'

A pause then: 'Very well, Jeremiah. If it's as important as that. I'll be right over. Give me ten minutes.'

He arrived exactly nine minutes later, stood inside the small hallway, shaking the drops of rain from his heavy coat. Calder closed the door behind him, shutting out the wind and the rain, which had begun again. Taking the other's coat, he hung it up on the rack, then led the way into the small front room where a fire was burning in the grate. He nodded towards one of the chairs.

'Sorry to drag you out on a night like this, Henry,' he said quietly, 'but I've just been up to see Charles Belstead.'

'Belstead?' The other looked surprised for a moment then nodded his head slowly, wisely. 'I think I'm beginning to understand. You wish to talk about him? Is that it?'

'Yes.' Calder spoke decisively. 'I went up there prepared to find him changed in some ways after his housekeeper died a little while ago. But I wasn't quite prepared for what actually happened there tonight.'

'All right, let's have it.' The other took the glass that the lawyer offered him and leaned back, resting his arms along the sides of his chair, stretching out his legs to their full length in front of him. 'What's on your mind as far as he's concerned. If you're worried about his sanity, I'll tell you here and now, that you're not the only one. I've been worried myself for a long time, but that's as far as it's gone.'

'Has he told you what happened forty-five years ago?'

The doctor paused, biting his lower lip. Then he nodded his head slowly, reluctantly. 'Yes, he told me that some time ago. I didn't believe him then and I'm not so sure that I believe him now.'

'Then how do you explain it? Imagination, and hallucination — or did he just make the whole story up to spite his father?'

'The last hypothesis is as good as any to my mind.' Woodbridge sipped his drink slowly. 'Hate can often do strange things. Since his mother died, Charles Belstead lived under the almost complete dominance of his father. Even when he left home and started a life of his own, he was never utterly free of that influence. An evil thing, I feel sure. But it isn't completely unheard of in medical science.'

'My own opinion,' said Calder, 'for what it's worth, is that we ought to get him away from that house as quickly as possible. I know it won't be easy. He's an old man, set in his ways, and for some strange reason he seems to be determined to stay there. I was hoping that you might be able to help there.'

'I agree with everything you say. But what can we do? Short of having the old man certified and removing him forcibly from the house, we can do nothing, and at the moment, I'm very reluctant to take that particular course.'

'Can you suggest anything else?' Calder lifted his brows into a bar-straight line. 'I don't like the idea of leaving him there much longer. The house seemed to possess some strange kind of morbid hold over him and I'm afraid that something may happen if we let this go on too long.'

Woodbridge got heavily to his feet and took a quick turn around the room. Pausing in front of the fire, he stared down at the other from beneath craggy, outjutting brows. 'Tell me, Jeremiah,' he said softly. 'Did Belstead ask you to go to the house tonight for any particular reason? It wasn't exactly the kind of night I would have chosen for a purely social call.'

'He talked a lot about various things, seemed to want to get them off his mind. But at the back of it all, I had the idea there was some other reason, although he never mentioned it.'

Woodbridge coughed uneasily, then turned and warmed his hands at the fire for a long moment without speaking. He seemed to be debating some point within himself. Calder waited patiently for the other to speak, knowing that he had something further to say. Pulling his pipe from his pocket, the doctor began to fill it with quick motions of his fingers, thrusting the unruly strands of tobacco into the bowl. Then he struck a match and inhaled deeply, flicking the spent match into the fire.

'How long is it since you last went into that house, Jeremiah? Before tonight, I mean?'

The other thought for a moment, then shrugged. 'Almost a year, I think. Why?'

'Before I answer that let me ask you one other question. Did you notice anything different there tonight — either with Belstead himself, or in the house?'

'I'm not sure what you mean. He seemed to have aged a lot since I last saw him, but I put it down to the strain of living alone, having to fend for himself. As to the house, there was dust everywhere, as if it had been utterly neglected since the house-keeper died. But neither of these things struck me as odd at the time.'

'And that's *all* you noticed?' The other's tone was strangely insistent.

'I — ' He paused abruptly. How to explain to a practical, scientific man like the doctor, what he had seen looking at him, through the door in the library?

'Go on. You did see something else, didn't you?'

'But how do you know that? Unless you too — '

Woodbridge gave a quick, jerky nod of his head, drew deeply on the pipe, pressing the tobacco deeper into the bowl. 'I called on Belstead less than a month ago. He asked me to go up and see him, thought there might be something wrong with his heart. I was there one afternoon. As soon as I saw him, I knew there was something wrong, but my examination told me it was nothing physical. Taking his age into account, his heart was in perfect shape. I tried to talk things out of him, but he was quite reticent and as soon as I suggested that he ought to pack up and leave the place, make the most of what life he still had left him, he almost bit my head off. It wasn't until I was leaving that I noticed the three people down by the lake. It was a clear, sunny afternoon, no question of bad light and shadows giving false impressions.' He paused, sucked on his pipe for a moment, then went on: 'You know that small boating house there is down by the lake. They were in there. I passed within twenty yards of them and I noticed them quite clearly. Time and again, I've been told that Belstead lived there alone, so it struck me as even more peculiar to notice anyone there at all.'

'Could you recognise any of them?' asked the other. In spite of the tight grip that he had on himself, Calder's tone was not quite steady.

'Only from the pictures I've seen,' went on Woodbridge slowly. 'One was old Doctor Talbot whose practice I took over when I first came here. His wife was with him and Colonel Carter.'

'Good God!' Stunned, shaking, Calder sat absolutely still, a sudden coldness on his face. He had almost known what was coming, but in spite of that, he found himself staring incredulously at the other, as if by staring, he could make it all sound completely impossible, make the other take back his words and say that he had been only joking. But it was not a joke, he told himself. His legal mind tried desperately to find some perfectly logical explanation for all that had happened. Those tales that the villagers whispered among themselves about what happened up at the Manor — just how much truth was in them, and how much had been exaggerated and fabricated?

'Now — you saw someone there, at the house tonight, who had no right to be there, didn't you? Was it one of those three?'

'No. It wasn't.' He twisted a little uneasily in his chair, then said with a grave quietness: 'It was Mister Peters.'

'The old solicitor you used to work for, forty years ago?'

'Yes. I'm quite sure of it. I know that it doesn't make sense. That all of these people we're talking about died many years ago. Yet we've both seen them up there at the Manor.'

'The rural tales are clear about what happens up at that old house,' said Doctor Woodbridge quietly. It was the following day, a morning of clear skies and flooding sunlight which made the horrors of the night before seem unreal and remote, so distant that to Calder's mind, it was almost as if they had never occurred. Woodbridge smoked for a moment reflectively, then continued: 'They might be queerer still if some of the things I've heard from a couple of my patients were brought out into the open.'

'What sort of things?' queried Calder uncertainly.

'I haven't mentioned this before to anyone, partly because it's so distasteful to recall, and also to protect the wishes of my patients. But I think, from what you told me last night and from my own experience a little while ago, that what I heard is relevant to this matter. Previously, I put all of this down to imagination, to the ramblings of two men who were not quite — rational, shall we say. In one case, I might even have gone further and said he was bordering on madness.'

'I promise to keep a straight face,' said Calder.

'Yes. I rather think that you will after you've heard what I have to say. Three years ago I was called out to one of the houses on the outskirts of the village a little after midnight. It sounded urgent so I'm afraid I broke any speed limits there might have been at that time of night and arrived at the house less than fifteen minutes after getting the call. By that time, the patient who was a youth of perhaps nineteen, was in a state of profound shock, bordering on hysteria. I did all I could for him, managed to calm him down and put him under mild sedation and then left, telling his parents to keep him in bed and I would call in to see him early the following morning. Unfortunately, there was an acute appendicitis case next morning and it was almost two in the afternoon before I got out to see him. He seemed to have recovered quite well from his experience and had a good grip on himself. I knew that something must have happened the previous night to shock him and I tried to get it out of him, knowing that if he would only talk about it, I might be able to help him a good deal. At first, he didn't want to say anything but from what little he did say, I got the impression that he had been up to the old Belstead place, probably poaching, and had either seen or heard something sufficiently frightening to have sent him running for home, shocked out of his wits.'

'What was your opinion about it?' asked Calder. Leaning forward, he filled the other's glass, then his own. The sunlight, flooding into the windows behind him made everything seem sane and normal, but the other's words had sent that strange and indefinable chill through him.

'At the time, I didn't have one.' The other seemed as if he did not quite trust himself to speak. 'I knew I had to get to the bottom of it, get the information from him as soon as possible, or there was a definite chance of him going insane.

Eventually, I got most of the story from him. Some of it seemed to have gone so far into his subconscious that nothing short of hypnosis could bring it to the surface. That — I left alone. He didn't expect anyone to believe a word of what he said, least of all a practical man like myself. And when he did tell me, I think I know why.'

Woodbridge closed his eyes for a moment and frowned in taut concentration as if trying to remember something, only to find it hard work, something he was not quite up to. 'According to his story, he had gone to the house about ten o'clock. It was an evening in late October and it was quite dark at that time with little moonlight, just enough to see by, but not bright enough for him to be seen easily. He apparently didn't believe the stories about the place and it wasn't until he was inside the grounds and moving towards the house that he noticed there was a certain feel about the place that he had not noticed before. It was nothing that he could describe to me. All he could say was that he felt something was going to happen that night and that when it did, it would be something hideous and frightening.' The doctor paused and sat down in his chair, his forehead furrowed. 'What happened then, according to him, was so unbelievable that at the time, I'm afraid I dismissed it completely as the ravings of a man on the borderline of hysteria. He approached the house from the hill at the back where the Belstead family are buried. It wasn't until he was going past the vaults that he saw where the iron gate had been pushed down — *from the inside.*'

'From the inside! But that's impossible.'

'I know. Now you can realise why I thought little about it at the time. Now looking back on it, I think it might have been possible to have averted a lot of what has happened since.'

'Go on,' prompted Calder.

'He found bits of torn cloth and dirt on the old pathway outside the vaults and being either a fool or a very brave man — I don't know which — he followed the trail that led almost directly to the library of the house. He said there were lights in the French windows, and at first, he thought it was candle-light but as he drew closer, he saw that it was something else — a weird, bluish glow that seemed to fill the whole room and spill out into the garden outside. It was a steady light, unlike the flickering of candle-light. Going closer, he looked inside.' A pause, then Woodbridge said in a clear voice: 'He discovered for himself, that the old Belstead house was not quite as empty as he had thought.'

'And you believe his story now?'

'Yes, I do. Since then, I've had a very similar story told me by a young servant girl who had to come past that place one night shortly before midnight. She saw lights in the house, bluish lights she described them, and figures outlined against the windows. Add to this what I saw with my own eyes that day I went up to see Charles Belstead, and what you claim to have seen yesterday and you'll see why I'm forced believe it.'

'But it goes against all reason.' Calder's logical solicitor's mind was trying to put a rational explanation on to all of this, and failing miserably. 'Is there any possible explanation for it?'

'I'm not sure. It must all tie in with old Henry Belstead. There seems to have been no talk of strange happenings there until he arrived in the house. Prior to that, everything was quite respectable.'

'I think I know what you're going to say,' went on the other quickly, 'and it's something I cannot accept. Such things just don't happen in this modern age,'

The other got to his feet, hands clasped behind his back. He spoke around the stem of his pipe thrust into his mouth. 'As a doctor, I have to examine everything in connection with any patients I have, no matter how strange it may seem at the time. As soon as I discovered what had happened to that boy I had to attend to, I started asking a lot of questions around the village, about things which happened before I arrived here forty or fifty years ago. At first, the folk here didn't want to talk about such things. They still look upon me as an outsider, even though I had been here for close on twenty-seven years. But gradually, they opened out and what they did tell me, made a very queer and bizarre sort of sense. Scientifically speaking, it makes no sense at all; because this deals with something which, at the moment, is quite outside of science as we know it; although there are a few men of vision in the States and elsewhere, experimenting with these metaphysical occurrences.'

'If you're trying to tell me that Henry Belstead is still alive, I can't believe you; and the same goes for the others. I was there at the reading of old Henry Belstead's will, and I can say quite confidently that he was dead then. He couldn't possibly be — '

The doctor shook his head slowly. 'How can I make you see?' he murmured. 'It never is very easy to explain these things. Sometimes, I think that because of our civilisation, we have regressed a long way from the senses which we had originally. The ancient peoples must have been a lot closer to the truth than we are. Now, we can't see these things because of the scientific facts that have built up a wall around them. And breaking through that wall is the most difficult thing in the world today.'

'So, all right, Henry Belstead started something and whatever it was, it still seems to be happening. What I want to know, is what's at the bottom of it all?'

'Black magic,' murmured the other. He emphasised the words queerly. 'You might say that this is something that went out of fashion by the middle of the Eighteenth Century.' He lowered his voice almost in apology. 'I suppose you could be forgiven for thinking that. Unfortunately, it doesn't happen to be true. As soon as I realised that there was something strange going on at the Belstead place, I took the trouble to read back over everything that was known about Henry Belstead.'

'And did you find anything? I should imagine you would find very little.'

'I found enough,' went on the other grimly. 'There was a little written about him in the local paper at that time, mostly from hearsay. But once I broke through the barrier of indifference, I managed to get quite a lot out of the people in the

45

village. It seems they have long memories when it comes to something like this.'

'These people talk about anything if they think they have found somebody willing to listen to them,' said Calder crisply. 'I've been a lawyer here for more than thirty-eight years and I think I can say that I know these people extremely well.'

Woodbridge shook his head slowly. 'But it's obvious that you didn't know Henry Belstead. If you had, you'd have realised that he was a very strange man.' He paused to let the full import of his words sink in. 'I can see that you don't believe that what you saw at the Belstead place the other night was anything out of the ordinary. You're confused and trying to make yourself believe that it was only someone who looked like old Peters and the bad light.'

'Well, I — ' He swallowed thickly, then went on hurriedly. 'I'm not sure now what I saw. I'm certain there was someone there. Who it was, I'm not prepared to say.'

'I can understand your attitude. This

46

isn't an easy thing to accept. You're a lawyer, and your legal mind always tries to seek a logical solution to everything. It was the same with me in the beginning. But there were too many little isolated incidents happened here, and when I collected them all together, and linked them up, I found that they made a strange kind of sense, a frightening kind of sense, but one which couldn't be ignored. I'm a doctor, Jeremiah. I believe in the things of the mind as well as of the body. Perhaps if I explained a little to you of what I discovered about Henry Belstead, you might begin to understand.' He lowered himself into the chair and leaned back, knocking out his pipe into the tray beside him, the ashes gleaming redly for a moment. 'Madness was in all of the Belsteads. I've recognised that from the beginning and I can prove that it was there from the middle of the Fourteenth Century. It must have been something to do with the family, because you'll find that there aren't many of them. Their family tree didn't put forth many branches, and the few that there are soon died out, leaving only the single line. Certainly, the madness came out in Henry Belstead when he was a younger man. He went off on long trips into the jungles of New Guinea, taking only natives with him. No white man would venture into the regions that he visited, but it was not until he came back and took up residence here that the talk really began. It was perhaps his own talk, especially when he was drunk, that led to the rumours so rife in the village later. I'm not surprised that the villagers thought him to be mad, when he talked of strange rites that were practised in the hidden jungles, of a power even stronger than voodoo and the ways these people had of raising the dead and other such hideous things.'

Calder uttered a sharp snort. 'And you're asking me to believe all of this? Good Lord, you're a doctor, you must know that these were just idle traveller's tales. There couldn't have been a word of truth in any of them.'

'You think so? If it is true that evil was practised in that house out there, a really potent brand of evil, might it not be that some of it still exists, some terrible force that had somehow been crystallised in the place, still able to exert some tremendous influence over anyone living there?'

Calder licked dry lips with a tongue that seemed suddenly to have gone stiff. Something that was lurking terror uncoiled itself in his mind. 'If you are right,' he said uncertainly, 'what can be done about it? Is there any way that it can be stopped before it gets out of hand?'

'I'm not sure. It all depends on how potent that force is.' The doctor spoke almost professionally, as if he were discussing a case with a patient. 'There are always ways of protecting yourself from these things. I'd already made up my mind to go there and see for myself — tonight.'

'But why at night?' He looked perplexed, bewildered almost.

'I'm afraid that you still don't fully understand, Jeremiah,' said the other gently. 'We aren't fighting things of flesh and blood and the powers that these things can command are not things that we can examine scientifically and catalogue for easy reference. These are the dark things of the night, the black knowledge of evil which has been sought throughout the long ages, discovered by only a few, and kept hidden. But all of the knowledge that has been gained is there for everyone to read if they only know where to look for it.'

'I see.' Calder nodded, no longer sure of himself. 'And what do you think will happen when you go? I only ask because I think someone should go with you and I'd like to know what to expect.'

'That's very difficult to say at the moment. If I knew, I'd feel a little easier in my mind.' Woodbridge grimaced slightly, then forced a smile.

* * *

Immediately, the silence settled down about the place. The moment they had stepped through the wrought-iron gate, the metal twisted into strange, cabalistic designs, closing it carefully behind them, it was as if they had, by that simple action, cut off all sound around them. Calder felt his taut muscles beginning to jerk spasmodically. He thought queerly that it was dreadful that any place could be so silent. Even the odour of the place had changed subtly but horribly, since he had last been there. Then there had been the smell of rain on wet leaves underfoot, of growing things — now there was an overpowering stench of cold, damp earth and stone.

It was impossible for Calder to describe the feeling that went through him at that moment as he stood there beside the doctor, staring into the cold, clammy darkness. The intense quiet had something to do with it, he felt sure — and that strange, sickly, cloying smell which persisted in his nostrils. Tensely, he found himself wishing that some sound would break in on that awful silence; the crush of their feet on the damp leaves beneath their feet on the gravel of the drive, thickly overgrown with weeds. But for what seemed an eternity, they stood absolutely still, feeling around with their eyes and ears, alert for the slightest

51

movement or the faintest sound.

Woodbridge turned his head. 'You're sure that you still want to go on with me?' His voice sounded eerie and unnaturally low in the clinging stillness. 'God only knows what will happen when we get there and I don't want you to — '

'I'll stay with you,' said Calder tightly. He could feel the coldness on his face and the muscles of his body seemed numb. 'I'm not sure what it is you expect to find up there.'

'Neither do I. But whatever it is, the sooner we know about it, the better.'

'Don't you think we ought to call the house first and see Charles Belstead? After all, I feel a little like a criminal walking through someone else's grounds like this, completely uninvited.'

'No.' Woodbridge's voice was harsh and decisive. 'That will do no good. I want to go through with the first part of this without him knowing anything about it. Besides, I'm sure that the evil emanates, not from the house itself, but from that place on top of the hill.'

They went forward into the dimness.

There was a moon lying low on the horizon, a great fiery red ball, touching the tops of the trees with a lurid glow like fire. He shivered. Ordinarily, he regarded the moon as a warm and friendly thing. Now there was fear in it, and terror. It was something strangely unreal and grotesque, abnormal, like a huge red eye that watched them from the heavens as they moved deeper into the trees, where they crowded in thickly on all sides, the shadows long and huge and dark. Calder glanced about him out of the corner of his eye, not quite knowing what to expect. The trees themselves did not seem quite right. The trunks looked too thick and grotesquely big for normal growth, with strange nodules sticking from their roots and the branches were twisted into ugly, fear-haunted shapes that clawed at the scudding clouds, almost, he thought inwardly, trembling a little, as if they were sucking something dark and poisonous from the ground.

He shrugged as he followed the tall shape of the doctor, pulling himself together. This was all part of his over-wrought imagination, he tried to tell himself fiercely. He was nervous and on edge. Jumpy. All of this running around the countryside on a night such as this, with a storm brewing somewhat on the western horizon, was not good for a man of his age. He shuddered convulsively for a moment and noticed that his hands were trembling more than usual.

The branches of the trees, twisted and gnarled, swept down against their faces and there was too much silence in them for Calder's liking. Over everything, there lay a curious sense of restlessness and unease, a haze of the grotesque and the unreal, as if something had been changed here, something which was not obvious at first glance, but which became more and more noticeable as they skirted the grounds and moved round towards the low hill at the rear of the house.

'This place is more than enough to give me the shivers,' muttered the doctor. His deep voice rumbled from the depths of his chest and he pulled the collar of his coat up higher around his neck.

'And yet young Belstead chose to stay

here rather than go away and enjoy himself with all that money he inherited,' said Calder tightly. 'I wish I knew why he did that. I'm certain that if we had the answer to that we might know what's behind all this.'

They moved out of the trees into the open. There was more of the yellow moonlight here but before them, where a narrow, muddy path led up the side of the hill, lay the dark vault where the Belstead family and their servants rested.

Instantly, they were more than ever aware of the silence. It seemed to shriek at their ears far more loudly and insistently than any sound. An almost tangible thing that was oppressive and heavy. Calder felt the sudden, almost physical impact of it the moment he stepped out of the trees and stood in the cold, musty air staring about him, rising tension in his mind.

His arms and legs felt numb and strange as if they were no longer a part of him.

The narrow pathway, muddy and running with moisture even though there had been no rain that day, led them up the side of the hill to the stone vault at the top. In daylight, it would have looked a morbid and dreadful place, but with that eerie moonlight falling upon it and faint muttering of the thunder in the distance, it brought a knot of fear to Calder's stomach as he stood a few feet away, unable to move any closer, while Woodbridge edged his way forward, his feet sliding on the smooth stone that surrounded the place. It had a look of age about it. There was a slimy kind of moss growing thickly on the walls, but it seemed significant that no other type of vegetation grew to within several feet of the low building. Almost, he thought inwardly, as if the other plants were deliberately shunning it.

He tried to pull himself together. There he went again, letting his imagination run away with him. There was nothing here they had to be afraid of, he told himself half-angrily. Those who rested inside this stone vault had been dead for many years and any idea that the dead could come back and harm the living was ludicrous.

All the same, he began to wish that he had not been so keen on coming with the other; and that he had accepted the chance back there at the gate and stayed behind, leaving the doctor to come out here on his own if he wanted to. After all, it had been Woodbridge's own idea to come to this godforsaken place and hunt around. What he expected to find here, Calder did not know. Certainly, it seemed unlikely that he would find the answers to any of the things that had been troubling him.

For a moment, outlined against the moonlight, Woodbridge stood in front of the iron gate which led into the vault. Calder heard his sudden exclamation and in spite of himself, went forward.

'What is it?' His voice seemed to rattle eerily from the rising stone walls.

'The gate — it's open.'

'Probably Belstead comes here sometimes.' Calder suggested. There was a strange dryness in his throat. 'Knowing him, it's hard to say what he gets up to at times.'

'No, it isn't that.' The doctor's cold

voice was muffled as he lowered his head. For a moment, there was a flash of light in the dimness as he flicked on the torch and flashed the beam in front of him. 'It's been broken open — and from the inside! See — the lock is still on the end of the chain.'

'But that's impossible.' He forced the words out through lips that were trembling a little. 'I mean — ' He wanted to enlarge on what he had said, but Woodbridge had flashed the beam of the powerful torch on to the ground and they both saw, quite clearly, the imprint of feet on the damp ground.

Calder's mind was a shrieking confusion of divided impulses, with the overriding one a dominant rush of fear. He wanted to turn and run, run back along that slippery winding path into the trees and then through the tangled undergrowth back to the gate and out onto the road where everything would be sane and normal again. But something held him rooted to the spot. His legs seemed paralysed, unable to move. Only his breath, rasping in his throat made any sound in the awful stillness. He felt like a man in a daydream, who knew that he was dreaming and yet could not awaken; repelled and at the same time oddly fascinated by what he saw. Then Woodbridge moved. He thrust himself forward with a muttered sound, whether oath or prayer it was impossible for Calder to determine, and disappeared inside the dark opening. The lawyer stood quite still outside, listening to the other moving around inside the dark tomb of the vault, saw the flashes of the torch as the other flicked the beam around the dripping, putrescent walls.

From where he stood, he could see the grossly distorted outlines of other things shadowed upon the walls and although he wanted desperately to close his eyes and yell at the other to come out, he could not do so. There was the inescapable feeling that no matter what had happened already, worse was still to come and the realisation unnerved him. It seemed an eternity before Woodbridge came out into the moonlight again and the expression on his face was one that Calder could not define.

'What is it?' he asked thinly. 'Is there something wrong in there?'

'There is.' Woodbridge put up his right hand to his eyes as if to wipe away the image of something he had seen. 'It's worse than I thought. We have to go up to the house right away if we are to stand any chance at all of stopping them.'

'But what is it?' Calder managed to get the words out before the other came forward, seized him by the arm, and pulled him, unresisting, along the path, back in the direction of the house, just visible beyond the tall trees.

'I'll explain on the way to the house,' went on the other hurriedly. 'There isn't a moment to lose. Perhaps it may be too late already.'

* * *

It was almost midnight now. The moon was high in the sky, riding just above the storm clouds sweeping in from the west and although it had lost its lurid red colour, the house seemed to pick something out of the moonlight, to transmute it into something terrible and evil. The broken chimneys stretched up like hands to the heavens and the eyeless sockets of the windows staring intently along the twisting drive towards the road.

This was how it had been for more than forty years, a place of dark and lonely shadows; and if there were lights and noises from the rooms, the villagers, passing on a cold November night, merely crossed themselves and hurried on, praying that the locks were strong on the gates of the vaults atop the hill, caring little of what might be happening to Charles Belstead, alone in that house with whatever horrors that might be beside.

Now, on that particular night, there was a peculiar waiting quality over it. The rooms were not empty and Charles Belstead was not alone. There were shadows in the house, eldritch things, the apotheosis of the unnameable. On the floor of the library at the rear of the house, the strange cabalistic designs glowed with an eerie, devilish light. There *was a flickering inside the room as of corpse candles, a cold radiance, a manifestation of the aura of evil that had never left the place, which was crystallised inside its very walls . . .*

★   ★   ★

As they came out of the trees onto the edge of the rambling lawn, the moon was swallowed up by the storm clouds, which had been moving in from the west, covering most of the sky. A few stars still showed to the north, but soon they too, would be engulfed by the blackness. There was a vivid flash of lightning just beyond the trees, followed a few seconds later by the titanic crash of thunder almost overhead.

'There's a light of some kind in the library,' said Calder tightly, clenching his teeth to prevent them from chattering in his head. 'Perhaps Charles is still up. At least, nothing seems to have happened here.'

'I only hope to God you're right,' muttered the other grimly. He took something from the pocket of his overcoat and held it tightly in his right hand. In the faint light, Calder saw that it was a small, golden crucifix. 'We mustn't go rushing in there with our eyes shut, trusting to blind luck to protect ourselves. I know these things and we can, at least, protect ourselves with the few things we have.'

Woodbridge did things that Calder did not understand, and all the time, the house stood brooding less than fifty yards away and the thunder mounted in intensity over their heads like some wild animal. Carefully, they moved along the narrow gravel path, which led around the lawn, at times stepping off it to walk on the grass verge so that their feet made no sound in the stillness. Calder shivered. Although he knew these grounds reasonably well, having visited the house on several occasions, somehow on this particular night, everything seemed altered and the memory of what they had found on the hill gave him the unshakeable impression that dreadful fear and possibly something worse dwelt in the house that night. The most innocuous details of the place seemed to possess a nightmarish appearance as the moon appeared in fitful glimpses through the thickening cloud.

★　★　★

Never before, had the presence of evil oppressed him so much as it did then. Here, he felt, was some blasphemous abnormality from the nethermost reaches of Hell itself, something evil which had been frozen into that house many years before, which defied time, and still lurked there, watching and waiting. And where, in God's name, did Charles Belstead fit into all this? Why had he never set foot outside the place ever since that day he had come home from his father's funeral? What kind of hold had this place got over him? The night suddenly grew hideous with things which were beyond all human comprehension and imagination.

They saw the lights in the library more clearly as they reached the corner of the house. Calder sucked in a harsh breath.

Was that a darker shadow just inside the large French windows — or was his overwrought imagination playing more tricks with him? He screwed up his eyes in reflexive instinct, then shook his head slowly almost to convince himself. Whatever it had been, it had seemed so intangible that it might never have existed.

They paused outside the windows, looking in. At first, Calder could see nothing. Then he made out the figure of Charles Belstead, seated in the tall, high-backed chair in front of the fire in the wide hearth. The flames had burnt down low, and there seemed to be only a faint spark still kindled there. But there was plenty of light in the room; a bluish glow that seemed to come from every corner of the library. It was an eerie, hellish glow that sent more shivers coursing up and down his spine. His hands were clenched tightly by his side, the nails biting deep into the palms, but he scarcely noticed. An unearthly chill seemed to reach through the glass of the windows and engulf him, numbing his muscles and limbs, swirling and eddying about him like something tangible, as a cold river current suddenly chills a man plunging into the water.

'We have got to go inside and face them.' As if from a great distance, the doctor's words reached him. A moment later, all sound was drowned by the peal of thunder that rumbled over their heads, crashing away to the horizon.

He saw the shadows in the room now — vague, half-seen things that vanished whenever he tried to look directly at them. A cold sweat of terror broke out on his forehead as he went forward slowly, behind the other. Woodbridge paused for only a moment, then thrust the large windows open and stepped through into the room. Swiftly, he raised the golden crucifix in his right hand as he strode forward, intoning something in a language that Calder did not understand.

A faint, low moaning sound began to make itself heard. Slowly, it rose in volume, striving to drown out the words Woodbridge was speaking. Out of the corner of his eye, he glimpsed his companion's face, drawn and white in that hellish glow. Sharply, he drew in his breath. In front of him, Charles Belstead, his face wrinkled like that of a mummy, suddenly lifted his head, stared at them with a strange expression on his face. For a moment, he seemed almost relieved, the tight lines on his features melting away swiftly. He got stiffly to his feet, made as if to move towards them with one arm outstretched, then stumbled forward like a man hit with a blackjack, spun halfway round on his heels, then went down quickly, arms outflung, fingers just touching the little silver cups, filled with some clear liquid, that rested at the corners of the glowing pentagram.

Without hesitation, Calder went forward, down on one knee beside the other. He forced himself to ignore the savage, exultant cry that rang through the room, something blended of triumph and horror, forced himself to ignore the sudden stab of pain in his body as the sound hammered at his ears. The flickering light in the room dimmed.

He felt for the old man's pulse, then

gently lowered his arm. It did not require Woodbridge to confirm that the old man was dead. He lifted his head to glance up at the other, shivered as an icy blast of air swirled around his kneeling body, chilling him to the bone. The room seemed to flicker and sway in front of his staring eyes. For a long moment, the walls, the pentagram on the floor, the books in their glass-fronted cases, seemed to glow with a weird and hellish light. By it, he could just make out the dim figures standing on the very edge of the designs etched into the floor. One, he recognised instantly as Charles Belstead and even as common sense told him that this could not be possible, that the other was lying dead on the floor in front of him, the body already growing cold under his fingers, he recognised the others. Henry Belstead, the lean saturnine face grinning eerily in the dimness, watching him from out of baleful eyes. Old Peters standing a little to the rear, his form as substantial as it had been in life. The old housekeeper who had died some seven years before. He knew that he had to turn and run, that somewhere Woodbridge was waiting for him, although he did not know where. A shrilling, evil laughter bubbled up from in front of him, joined by other voices that he did not recognise, until the sound shrieked along the endless corridors of the house, blending in the end into one vast peal of thunder that seemed to shake the building to its very foundations.

It was then that he knew he was lost. That this was what Woodbridge had been afraid of, that the utter evil which had originated in the house all those years before, when Henry Belstead, using the terrible knowledge that he had gained during his long travels into the jungles of New Guinea, had brought forth terror and a diabolical madness in return for some strange form of immortality of his own.

He could feel the sweat beginning to run down the folds of his cheeks and the muscles of his arms and legs jerked spasmodically without his control. His face twitched uncontrollably. There was no sign of Woodbridge; but it was difficult to see anything clearly in that terrible room. With an effort, he got to his feet and groped blindly forward. Another peal of thunder, a vivid flash of lightning outside the windows. Then something seemed to snap inside his brain and he pitched forward on to his face, knowing nothing.

★   ★   ★

Jeremiah Calder woke with a start, his mind hazy as it forced its way out of unconsciousness. His body felt cold, his limbs numbed. His arms and legs moved stiffly and jerkily, like those of a puppet caught on strings. In the dim light, he managed to make out the large bookcase over against the wall, the fire in the wide hearth, now dim and grey, little more than a heap of ashes; and the tall French windows open to the dawn.

Afraid, startled, he pulled himself to his feet. His heart was thumping madly against his ribs although, at the moment, he was not sure why. Something had happened he told himself hazily, something that he did not understand. He recalled coming to this place with Woodbridge the previous night, during that terrible storm, and of what they had discovered up there on the hill when they had visited the family vaults. Then they had made their way here and —

His thoughts gelled inside his head. Had he really seen all those terrible creatures in this room? Was Charles Belstead really dead? And if so, where in God's name was the doctor who had accompanied him here?

Outside, it was almost dawn. The storm had evidently moved away when he had been unconscious. Already, there was a clearing in the east and the trees stood outlined against it. He shivered, pulled the coat more tightly about his body. There was no sense in a man of his age staying here any longer now. Somehow, he had to find Woodbridge and discover what had happened. Perhaps he might find out that it had all been a dream.

He rubbed the muscles on the back of his neck, moved towards the library door. Then he paused. Another door opened somewhere in the near distance. He heard the eerie creak of rusty hinges and felt the cold draft on his body a few seconds later. The mere sound of that door opening slowly made him shiver convulsively and his teeth began to chatter in his head. He turned on his heel, ran to the French windows. They were closed, yet he distinctly remembered that a few moments earlier they had been lying open. Perhaps that draft he had felt, had blown them shut and he had not noticed it, he told himself, twisting the handle, he tried to open them. A second later, terrified beyond anything he had ever known, he was tugging desperately at them as they stubbornly refused to open. He felt like screaming out aloud with the terror that bubbled up inside him. Outside on the lawn, through the glass, he caught the glimpse of a dark shadow that stood under the trees, watching him with red eyes. Henry Belstead!

He whirled with a cry, ran to the door and jerked it open, out into the corridor and through the room at the other end, running to the front door. The chain slipped in his fingers as he fumbled with it. Then he headed out. Savagely, seized with a desperate strength, he jerked open the door, made to run out into the drive, then stopped abruptly as Charles Belstead stepped out of the trees, glided on to the drive and moved towards him. Hurriedly, frenziedly, he slammed the door shut, leaned back against it, trembling violently, shaking fingers up to his mouth. More sweat popped out on his forehead and the horror suddenly washed over him afresh. That loathsome thing outside — and the other on the lawn at the back of the house; and God alone knew where those other abominations were.

Very slowly, still shaking uncontrollably, he made his way back into the house. A lot of things made sense now; a crazy, terrible kind of sense. He knew why Charles Belstead had never left this house, even when he had all of that money, when everyone expected him to go back to his riotous life in London. The evil that had once been brought into this terrible house was still there. And Charles Belstead, old and afraid, could not be allowed to die until there was someone there to take his place. He tried to control the shivering in his limbs. No matter by which way he tried to get away, there would always be one of those creatures waiting for him, preventing him from leaving. What had happened to Doctor Woodbridge he did not know. Whether the other was still alive or not, was something he might never know. He went back into the library, feeling the coldness in the room.

It came as no surprise to him, when old Mr. Peters stepped through the wall and stood smiling down at him.

2

The Seventh Image

There was a thin spatter of rain against the window. Down in the hall, the grandfather clock gave several desultory chimes; eight booming echoes that chased themselves up the winding stairs.

Over by the window, Peter Kennett stared down at the darkening trees and pathways through the dull washing of rain. Night was moving through the sky with an ominous, relentless surge of racing storm clouds. A chill wind moaned drearily around the house, rattling the sash of the window with icy fingers. He turned away and then looked down again at the letter in his hands.

But it still read the same, fingering little thrills of fear up and down his back, though he didn't quite know why. The words seemed to thrust themselves at him, commanding attention, burning their way into his brain.

And yet, on the face of it, it was nothing more than a very ordinary letter. He forced himself to read it again:

Dear Peter,

Remember we were talking about Arnold Kestro the other day during lunch? I gathered from what you said then, that he was a pretty elusive fellow to get to know. Probably this will surprise you then. I've managed to get myself an invitation to a dinner he's giving tomorrow night.

He seemed to me to be quite a friendly person, nothing out of the ordinary, and not at all unusual. A little odd in his ideas perhaps, but that's all.

I'll be going down there about eight o'clock, but I'll call in and see you on the way. Perhaps you'll be able to tell me a little more about him before I go.

Regards,

James.

Savagely, Kennett crumpled the thin sheet of paper in his hand and flung it into the centre of the room. The fool! his mind yelled at him. The blind, utter fool!

The writing looked simple and clear enough, but unlike many others, he was able to read between the lines, to see what lay at the back of it all. He lit a cigarette with a sudden flick of his lighter, and blew a ring of swirling smoke angrily into the air.

Kestro! Arnold Kestro! The name sent a little shiver of apprehension through him. Probably the most infamous name in the whole history of the Black Art. And James Fisher was walking unwittingly, unbelievingly, into a hell from which there would be no return.

It wasn't that he had anything against Kestro, he told himself inwardly. All he knew about the man he had heard from others. Not once had he met him face-to-face. To look him straight in the eye and say to himself: This man is an enemy of all that is good and decent and sane in the world.

Several years had passed now since he

had first begun his single-handed campaign against these fiends in human guise who continued to prey on the frailty of Man. In the beginning, it had all been quite fascinating, even fun, this tampering about with the black forces of evil, the unknown.

But the novelty and the fascination wore off in a hurry. When one saw the brutality and the misery and the horror that came with it. The madness and the sinister nightmare that existed on the Other Side.

The hollow-eyed things that had once been men and women, meeting in tiny secret groups, away from their fellow creatures, shunning the light, mumbling their frenzied words of idolatry, indulging in mind-shuddering orgies of sheer bestiality. Sure it existed. And as long as it did, he would go on fighting it.

Something had gotten him over the weary years. It was more than a battle now, it was a crusade. He could always tell himself that when everything else failed. When the madness and screaming fear and the panic came padding in on noiseless feet.

Then it was necessary for someone to step in and say: Stop! This is enough! He smiled grimly to himself and turned back to the middle of the room. That was the magic word, the charm that made everything so fine and correct. Even when you knew, deep down inside, the proper thing to do was to leave them to stew in their own juice. To sink deeper into the hell of their own making.

There was a sudden sound outside, above the incessant patter of rain on the grass. A car turned into the drive. Headlights threw the entire room into harsher brilliance as they swung momentarily over the window.

That would be Fisher coming to see him. He tightened his lips and squared his thin shoulders. A lot would depend on whether he could persuade the other not to go, to turn down this devilish invitation. If he couldn't —

His mind stopped there because he could see no other way out. A car door slammed outside in the teeming rain. Feet pounded up the steps to the front door. A moment later, he felt the slight draft as it was pushed open.

That was Jimmy, all right. He'd been coming here so often now that he never bothered to knock. The other's deep bass voice reached him from the bottom of the stairs.

'Peter! Where are you, you old devil-worshipper?'

The same old Jimmy, he told himself for the second time. He opened the door of his room and stood in the square of light at the top of the stairs.

'Up here, Jimmy. Come on up.'

'Thought you were out, Peter.' The other came running up the stairs, two at a time, as he always did, the yellow light shining faintly on his wide features with the dark blue eyes dominating everything else, seeing no evil in the world. That was the trouble, thought Kennett bitterly.

The other refused to believe in the existence of devils and other things of the darkness. Which was obviously why he had received this invitation to dinner.

'You got my letter, I see. I didn't want

to go without having another little talk with you. You were quite wrong about Kestro, Peter. Really you were. All that Black Magic stuff.'

Kennett let him ramble on, leading him gently into the room. A tiny corner of his mind was listening attentively to what the other was saying, but the rest was spinning madly inside his head.

How to stop him from going? Keep him here by force?

He looked at the other out of the corner of his eye, as he mixed a couple of drinks, and shook his head slightly. Tall, athletic, well-built, James Fisher had always been the outdoor type, all the time he had known him.

A complete contrast to his own slight build, and more studious nature. Possibly that was why they had always got on well together. Mutual liking of opposites. No, he decided, he wouldn't be able to keep the other here by force, even if he were foolish enough to try.

He walked over to where the other sat, quite at ease, in the high-backed chair in front of the blazing fire. 'Here,' he said.

'Take this. It'll bring some of the heat back into you. God! You must be frozen after driving through that.'

He inclined his head to where the rain was still spilling sheets against the window. Lightning threw a blue sheet of flame across the world, outlining the wind-tossed trees that threshed wildly against the sky. The dull rumble of thunder came an instant later, booming about the walls like an insane thing, venting its anger on the world.

Fisher had the drink in his hand but did not immediately partake of it. His face was full of an uneasiness that Kennett noted and didn't like.

'It would seem that you have already made up your mind to go to Kestro's place tonight,' he said suddenly, breaking the uncomfortable silence. God! What was coming over them? He had never felt ill at ease with Fisher before. He sat down and sipped his drink.

'That's rather obvious, old man.'

Kennett bit his lip. 'I'd rather you didn't go, Jim,' he said sharply, blurting the words out. 'If only you knew what you were letting yourself in for, I'm sure you'd think twice about accepting that devilish invitation.'

'Peter,' said the other, leaning forward, a smile on his face. 'You've been mixing with devils and black magic for so long now, you see it where it doesn't exist. You seek inhuman shapes lurking in every corner. You even read things into a normal, simple, everyday invitation that aren't there. I remember what you said about Arnold Kestro the other day, and I have no doubt that you believed it all quite sincerely. But this is London, man. In the middle of the twentieth century.'

'And what difference do you think that makes?' muttered Kennett with a sharpness beyond his intention. He felt suddenly on edge. 'The worship of the Devil is as old as Christianity, at least. Probably older. And you wouldn't say that that had died out, would you?'

'No. But — '

'There are two sides to every road, Jim. Just as there are two sides to life itself. The black and the white. Good and evil.

Both of them are always with us, and both are forces to be reckoned with. Believe me, I'm not speaking without some knowledge of the subject. If you'd seen as much horror and pain as I have and as much terror as I've been through, you'd realise why I'm trying to keep you from that place tonight.'

Fisher rumbled out a loud laugh. But the other detected a faint, forced quality about it. 'So because you studied these things, you actually credit their existence? Well, I won't argue with you. I suppose you know what you're saying. But coming from anyone else, I'd have to say they were mad. All I'm saying is that I know Arnold Kestro. I've spoken with him, studied him, watched his movements, met some of his friends. And I can see no evil in the man.'

'And so,' went on Kennett slowly. 'You intend to go out there, to disregard my warning.'

The other spread his hands in a gesture of resignation. 'What else can I do, Peter? I can quite see your point. But I can't simply refuse to go, just because you don't like the man. What would they think?'

'It would appear,' muttered Kennett in a quiet, ominous voice, 'that what they think of you matters a lot more than what they can do to you.'

'How do you mean?'

'You're walking straight into trouble if you go to that dinner, Jim. Bad trouble. And I'm not joking.' There was a chill in his voice, hard and brittle, like ice.

'Nonsense,' said the other. He seemed a little shaken but there was a new look of determination on his face, that Kennett hadn't noticed before.

'Just because you're obviously afraid of the fellow, it doesn't mean to say that I am.' He stood up. 'To hell with all your imaginary devils, Peter. I'm going to that dinner at Kestro's and nothing is going to stop me. And I'll come back — and in the morning I'll come round to see you and laugh at your fear and stupid superstitions.'

'Then you've made up your mind to go despite anything I can say?'

'Certainly.' Fisher nodded his head

emphatically. 'I refuse to run away from these things of the dark that exist only in people's overwrought imagination. I don't believe in them, and until I see them for myself, I refuse to credit the fact that they exist.'

'You'll see them soon enough.' Kennett reached for the heavy overcoat that lay neatly folded over the back of a nearby chair, waiting. He pulled it on and buttoned it up above the neck. Then he walked towards the wooden rack where his hat lay among the sticks and umbrellas. The other watched him in surprise.

'Why the coat?' he asked finally.

Kennett regarded him steadily a few moments before speaking. Then he said quietly: 'Because since you refuse to accept my advice to stay away from this place, I consider it my duty to come with you. Perhaps, by being there, I may be able to divert some of evil that is sure to come of this meeting.'

'But you can't come.' His companion cleared his throat, fighting down his surprise. 'You've received no invitation.

How will you get in?'

The other nodded slowly. 'A good question,' he said. 'But I doubt very much whether our Mr. Kestro will want to make a scene by having me kicked out. Not tonight, anyway. Don't worry, I'll get in all right. And I intend to stick to you like glue for the rest of the evening.'

Fisher shrugged his broad shoulders. It was a purely reflex gesture. 'Well — that's up to you entirely. I wish I could just make up an excuse like that every time I wanted to gatecrash a society dinner.'

'This time, I'm afraid it's absolutely necessary,' muttered Kennett. He switched off the light and led the way down the stairs.

'But you're mad if you think you can pull it off.'

'Perhaps. But in a case like this, it's better to be mad than to allow these things to take place. Maybe you don't know it, and you won't believe it, but when you met Kestro the other day you met someone who is definitely a representative of those forces of evil, I was speaking about at lunch. Oh, I know you'll say I'm insane to think such things. No one in their right mind believes in supernatural forces these days. It just isn't done. But you met some of them — and tonight, unless I miss my guess, you're going to meet some more. And this time, they'll be the real ones. Kestro, for all his evil power, is just a puppet for them.'

'*Them?* You mean vampires and demons and things like that?'

'Maybe. Though you're being a little specific. But that's the term used for them today.' He opened the door of the car and slid himself inside, slamming it behind him.

Rain drummed steadily on the roof, streaming down in tiny rivulets over the windscreen. The drive in front of them was a mirror-like stretch of water. Fisher slipped in beside him. The engine started with a faithful-throated roar that was somehow comforting to hear.

They discussed the matter for a little while as the car headed out of the city into the more open country roads. And then, finally, a sort of impatience crept into their tone, and they relapsed into a silence broken only by a muttered sentence or two.

Fisher drove the car with a restless abandon, keeping his foot down on the accelerator, peering ahead into the well of darkness that seemed to open out momentarily to let them pass, to slide over them in a river of midnight; and then close in behind the car as if trying to block any way of return.

Twenty minutes later, they came within sight of the old house that stood a little way back from the main road, half-hidden by a veritable barricade of tall trees, as if trying to hide itself away from prying eyes.

Fisher swung the car through the massive, wrought-iron gates. There was the sudden crunch of gravel beneath the wheels. Kennett leaned forward in his seat and peered through the windscreen. It was always best, when going into anything like this, to get an idea of the layout of the place.

There was no telling when they would have to move fast to get away. And past experience had taught him never to overlook a single thing.

The rain had stopped its insane lashing and there was a thin crescent of a moon racing through the tattered wisps of cloud. The mansion that showed clearly for the first time as they rounded a bend in the road, seemed to repel him at once.

Tall, twisty towers ripped the sky, clawing defiantly for the moon. There were lighted windows in the face of it, like a hundred hungry eyes, staring and vacant, watching their approach.

For an instant, looking at it, the fear was strong within him. Then, consciously, he pushed it down and tried to ignore it, although it was still there, just below the surface, ready to spill over him in a single instant, should the opportunity arise.

They drew up in front of the house, into the sudden harsh glare of light from the porch. A single glance was sufficient to show Kennett that most of the other guests had arrived. There were several cars lined up along the drive.

Together, they walked up the wide, cold marble steps. Kennett felt his teeth beginning to chatter in his head. And there was a warning tingle along his nerves. It had all begun again. Once more he was bringing himself face-to-face with evil.

There was a touch of the exotic and the Oriental about the place, he decided, which must be why —

He grew aware that they had reached the open door. Somebody was standing with his back to the light, watching him. Arnold Kestro! He caught a glimpse of fat, smoothly rounded cheeks and small narrow eyes, very black and cruel, beneath almost non-existent brows.

A huge, balding head was balanced almost precariously on top of the body, which although grotesquely fat, still seemed too small for it.

Kestro extended a hand to him, warm and moist. 'I understand you are a friend of Mr. Fisher's. You are most welcome to the little dinner I am giving. I regret he didn't tell me about you earlier, or I could have sent a formal invitation.'

Was there a touch of hidden menace in the other's thick, oily voice? A definite beat of sarcastic laughter? Kennett wasn't sure. He nodded, bowing slightly from the waist.

'I trust you'll pardon the intrusion,' he said as calmly as he could. 'But my friend happened to mention he was coming here, and I — '

'But think no more of it, my friend. All are welcome. The more the merrier.' He turned away with a wave of a thick hand, to greet someone else coming up the steps behind them.

The more for what? thought Kennett grimly. More souls to offer to their evil master? It seemed unlikely, but even so, it was something he didn't want to think about. Not at the moment, anyway.

He gave his overcoat and hat to the tall, muscular Creole standing silent, watchful, just inside the door.

He grew aware that his companion was speaking again. 'There, Peter. What's wrong with Kestro? Even you've got to admit there's nothing evil in him. Oh, I know he looks a little sinister. But that isn't his way. Believe me, you've nothing to worry about. Though I must admit I'm rather glad you decided to come. I hardly know a soul here.'

'There are no souls here,' said Kennett, but he didn't say it aloud. He glanced about him. The room was well and tastefully furnished, almost to the point of extravagance. And the guests, already present, went with the room.

But then, that was nearly always the case. These people were not confined to the poor, the ignorant. They came from all levels of society and, obviously, Kestro confined his attentions to the highest levels.

Possibly, he thought, there was more money in that way. Because, in spite of everything, funds were always needed for their activities. He turned sharply to find Kestro standing at his side. There was an expression of diabolical amusement in the other's dark eyes, which vanished as soon as he turned.

'Forgive me for neglecting you both,' he said skilfully. 'But I keep forgetting you're new here. All the others are all friends, very old friends indeed.' He looked from Kennett to Fisher, then back again. 'Perhaps you'd both like a drink. I have some very good whiskey, if you care for it. Just come this way.'

He showed them into a small, warmer-looking room that opened off the main hallway by means of a short, curved corridor. But in spite of the warmth and the comfort that the room tried, almost painfully, to thrust upon the eye, Kennett could sense the presence of something else.

Something thick and unclean, black and evil, that spread outwards from the brightly-papered walls. As if death had been a constant visitor there, coming here many times, but never staying for very long.

He took the drink the other offered him with a feeling of sinking fear in the pit of his stomach. His keen gaze flicked round, suddenly wary. Out of the corner of his gaze, he could see that Fisher was nervous too. He sipped his drink with quick, jerky motions and there was a grey bleakness about the fine lines of his face.

'You should both feel a little honoured to be here, gentlemen,' said Kestro, mopping his face with a red, square handkerchief. 'It isn't often I show my inner sanctum to people the first time they come.'

For some time, Kennett peered about him curiously, trying to locate the source of the evil he could feel, crowding around him, hemming him in with dark fingers. He had worked and fought against it for too long now to be mistaken. Evil usually associated itself with some object or collection of objects. And where those objects went, there would go the evil also.

And this time, there was a malignant quality about it he had seldom felt before. *Horror is lurking here*, mumbled his mind; *waiting for a chance to reach out and destroy you.*

He caught at himself savagely. Desperately, he pushed calmness into his mind to replace the rising fear that he found there. There were several things strewn about the room, seemingly carelessly, but to his trained mind there seemed a motive behind everything. A method and an arrangement that lay half-hidden below the surface.

Carved bits of wood and stone, shaped

into grotesque figures, dreamed up by the twisted mind of a madman. Tiny miniatures of idols and a brown skull that grinned down at him with a sightless stare from the top of a dark cupboard.

His mind flicked back, withdrawing a little into itself. He turned his head slightly. Those tiny idols. Surely they were —

'Ah, so you've finally spotted my little images,' muttered Kestro, easing his huge bulk forward. 'Cleverly fashioned, aren't they? Take a close look at them. I'll guarantee you've never seen anything quite like them in your travels, Mr. Kennett.'

The other stepped forward, chilled by a sudden thought. Just how had the other known that he had travelled? His brain quietened. Jimmy had told him, of course. That was the only explanation.

Six tiny figures. Each exquisitely made, every detail perfect; down to the folds in the clothes, even to the individual expressions on their faces.

God! And what expressions they were! As if they had been forced to look at things that were not fit for human eyes to see, just at the moment of their death. He bent his head, fascinated.

For a brief moment, it almost seemed as if they were somehow alive, breathing quietly, watching him with a mute pleading on their lips. But that was impossible. A trick of the dim light. With an effort, he threw off the illusion of madness that threatened to overwhelm him, deliberately he pushed it out of his thoughts.

He mustn't let himself start imagining things. Because that was fatal. It slowed his mind and reflexes to danger point. And when the time came for them to get out of this place, if they ever got out, it would be necessary, not only to think fast, but to move fast also. Because they might never get a second chance.

'They're all very well made,' he agreed finally, fighting down his dislike of the man. He straightened his back and looked around. 'Where did you pick them up?'

Kestro smiled enigmatically, creasing the flabby folds of his face. 'Oh, that's my little secret,' he said in his oily tone.

'Perhaps one day, I may be able to tell you. But until then, I'm afraid — '

He spread his thick fingers in a gesture that had little meaning behind it, but Kennett thought he detected a definite beat of menacing laughter behind the other's words.

Then Kestro glanced up, almost guiltily, at the marble-edged clock on the wall. 'Forgive me for keeping you both talking like this. It's getting late and dinner will be ready. Perhaps we had better rejoin the guests.'

Dinner was a meal of silence, quickly over. Kennett ran his practiced gaze over the assembly and didn't like what he saw. It was if a vast cloud of darkness grew over the entire gathering, spread and spread, pressing down over the tall candles and silver sticks, making the leaping shadows climb jerkily out of the walls.

Weakly, he leaned back in his chair and tried to concentrate on what lay ahead. Around him, voices spoke in quiet little murmuring sounds, almost unheard, fading slowly, but nevertheless intruding on his consciousness sufficiently to wrench his mind away from what he was trying to think about. The tall candles threw a pale light upon him and the voices were scarcely whispers now in the great black shadow.

They seemed somehow to blend together into an oddly soothing sound, half-lulling him to sleep. He jerked upright in his chair, suddenly frightened. He mustn't let that happen! He looked round at the faces nearest him. Blurry wisps of whiteness around the table. And somehow, they all looked dead, as if part of them, some vitally essential part, had been taken away.

He grew aware that Kestro had risen to his feet at the end of the long, candle-lit table. He stood for a moment, surveying them all. Then he said quietly: 'I trust you have all eaten well, and that the food was satisfactory.'

Damn it! thought Kennett fiercely. *Why did the fellow always have to be so ingratiating?*

'Most of you here will know what comes next, my friends.' A hidden devil licked its lips hungrily behind the dark flames of his eyes, before falling back into the black depths. Then the heavy lids dropped lazily back into place.

There was a sudden scraping of chairs. Kennett pushed his back automatically and rose to his feet with a tense sensation of impending disaster in his body. The feast had ended; the madness and the horror was about to begin!

Fisher stepped closer to him. There was a worried frown on his lean face. His eyes were clouded.

'What the devil do you suppose he meant by that?' he asked.

The other tightened his lips convulsively. 'It's quite clear to me what he meant. This is where they prepare for the Black Mass. Or some other equally horrible service. It isn't going to be very nice to watch.'

He glanced about him, desperately, seeking a way out of escape. *Hurry! Hurry!* his mind shouted at him. *While there is still time.*

'We've got to get out of here somehow,' he said in whisper, speaking out of the side of his mouth. 'And fast! Once they start this fiendish sacrifice, there'll be no stopping them. And there's something else you probably ought to know.'

'What's that?' The other was visibly agitated. A little muscle in his cheek was jumping madly. And there was a pulse beating heavily in his neck.

'They need a victim — a human sacrifice, unless I'm very much mistaken.' He glanced at the other out of the corner of his eye, keeping most of his attention on the tall Creole in front of the main entrance. 'Something tells me, that's why you were invited in the first place,' he added significantly.

'Nonsense.' Fisher squared his shoulders, but there was a thin quaking in his voice that he couldn't hide.

'Still think he's just gathered these people here for a friendly game of bridge?' murmured Kennett grimly. He inclined his head towards the far end of the room. 'Then take a good look at that.'

Fisher turned. Two servants carried an oblong crate, half-filled with straw and something that moved and screeched, into the middle of the room. Kestro walked over from a nearby group of laughing guests and looked down at it carefully, examining the contents.

Then he nodded, evidently satisfied, and gave a quick jerk of a thick hand towards the door set in the wall, covered with a heavy drape of black cloth. His lips were moving, but he was too far away for either of them to make out what he was saying.

'See what was in that?' enquired Kennett tersely. His heart was beginning to hammer madly at the base of his throat. His brain felt oddly stiff. 'No. Then I'll tell you. A black cockerel and a pure white hen.' He clamped his teeth together, tight.

'They're not fooling this time. This is the real thing. Unless I miss my guess, Kestro intends to carry the Black Mass through to its completion tonight.'

The other ran his fingers worriedly through his mop of brown hair. 'What the devil do you mean?' he asked thinly, speaking half to himself.

'He intends to raise the Devil himself.'

'But that's — It's ridiculous.'

'Is it? I can assure you there's no trickery about this.' He took hold of the other's arm in a tight grasp. 'Whether you believe it or not, I'm getting you out of here. Come on — and try not to make it too obvious that we're leaving.'

They walked slowly towards the door, eyes wary, watchful. The Creole servant eyed them curiously as they approached, but said nothing and made no move to bar the way.

'I'm afraid we'll have to leave sooner than we expected,' said Kennett, forcing calmness into his voice. Whether the other understood what he said, he wasn't quite sure. 'Would you bring my hat and overcoat?'

The Creole turned away. There was an expression of grim, sardonic amusement at the back of his dark eyes that sent a convulsive shudder racing over Kennett's limbs. Something was wrong! He was positive about that. Surely they couldn't just walk out like this. It was almost as if —

'Oh, but you're not leaving so soon.' The oily voice sounded at his elbow. He whirled. Kestro stood a couple of feet away. There was a smile spread over his grotesque face, but the leaping devil was there in his eyes.

They regarded Kennett steadily, unblinking, like twin slivers of molten silver, shining faintly in the shadow of his face.

'Why the party has only just begun. You don't want to miss the most interesting part, surely?' A deep, chuckling gasp of sheer, unadulterated evil rippled and heaved his great, flabby bulk. His blue lips, almost engulfed in flesh, twisted into a sly grin.

His right arm reached out towards Kennett, found his sleeve and clung to it. There didn't seem to me much strength in the thick fingers, but the other could scarcely repress a shudder of revulsion as they touched him.

'I'm afraid I can't allow you to go without first witnessing my little — surprise — I usually keep in store for my guests.'

'Don't be a fool, Kestro! Do you think I'm so blind that I can't see what you're up to? I warned Fisher what would happen to him if he came here. But he wouldn't listen. That's why I accompanied him, as you've probably already realised.'

'True. You're a very clever man, Mr. Kennett, but a very foolish one. You realise that by coming here, you've delivered both yourself and your friend into my hands entirely.' He clapped his hands together sharply. 'Now we have two victims for the sacrifice to the Great Master. Two, not one.' His high laugh sent madness blazing like a flame through Kennett's mind, searing away all the emotion and the sanity. He couldn't think, his brain refused to function. 'Now you will both have to stay and see it through. Right to the very end.'

'What the devil — ' Kennett lunged forward. Arms grasped him tightly about the elbows, before he had taken a couple steps, holding him back. Madly, he struggled to free himself. God! Once these things got them into that accursed temple of theirs —

'You can't escape,' purred Kestro in a

low voice that was almost lost in the bloated throat. 'Every door is watched. Just try to remember that and give us as little trouble as possible.' His flabby face creased in a broad grin. 'It won't be long now. Already, the final preparations are being completed. Bring them into the temple.'

Something caught Kennett a wicked blow on the arm and a guttural voice from behind him muttered an unintelligible command. Almost instinctively, he stifled the gasp of pain that rose unbidden to his lips, and stumbled forward.

Out of the corner of his eye, he saw Fisher was receiving the same treatment. His mind was spinning like an unloaded engine, throwing up plan after unusable plan. They had to get out of this nightmare place. But how? It was something for which he had no answer at the moment.

Kestro came forward, his face very evil, and pushed aside the black drapery revealing a narrow door set deep into the wall. He unlocked it with a key from his pocket and motioned them inside.

Kennett stepped through with Fisher following close on his heels. Then he halted in mid-stride, all the fear coming back like a cold hand clutching at his heart, speeding it up, gripping the muscles of his chest.

The first impression that forced itself on his dazed mind was — blackness! The room was long with a low ceiling and even the walls were black, smooth and shiny. Black tapestries, embroidered with the ancient symbols of the Order of Sathanas hung everywhere.

At the far end was a vast altar, a thing of black marble, surmounted by a huge broken Cross being crushed in the coils of a gigantic black serpent. Black candles of pitch stood on either side, flickering dimly in the darkness.

The altar cloth was embroidered with gold, studded with precious stones that winked mockingly at Kennett, jeering at him out of a thousand eyes of blue and red and green; depicting scenes from the Book of Set.

And in front of the altar, rising from the cold smoothness of the temple floor, was a rough stone slab, badly discoloured with dark stains that time could not efface.

Kennett felt his body tighten. God alone knew how many poor wretches had been sacrificed on that bloody stone slab to appease some hideous Black Deity, butchered by a crazy priest such as Kestro.

'You had better prepare yourselves, my friends. Tonight the Great Master receives two more victims, and I make myself one with the Dark One. Then, everything will be mine.' Kestro moved forward until he stood in front of them, glaring up with a feral eagerness on his massive features.

His face seemed to lift from his body, to float all by itself, outlined against the grey dimness. But the oily smile was still there and the small eyes looked steadily into his, staring down into his very soul.

Kennett steeled himself. This loathsome monster in human guise must not overcome him, or they were both lost. The darkness seemed to shimmer and recede, the walls of the black temple to flow away until they stood in a far distance. Kestro's gaze locked with his.

His face loomed closer. And now there was something black and awful around it, an evil aura that seemed intent on leaping forward at him with a frenzied movement, falling back only as he strove to keep a tight hold on his buckling consciousness.

Finally, when it seemed his mind could hold out no longer, normality returned.

The black walls rushed back into their original places, and there was Kestro, his head rejoined to his grossly corpulent body, glaring down at him. Then, without another word, he brushed past them, out through the narrow door, slamming it behind him. *They were alone in the Temple of the Damned!*

Kennett started forward between the long rows of seats, his face taut. 'There must be some way out of here,' he said fiercely. 'There has to be. If only we can find it before that hellish crew comes back.'

They went down into the lower levels of the temple towards the crazy altar with its symbols and evil-smelling candles. At the back, there was an elaborately-carved handrail, winding away through the heavy darkness.

'What's this?' asked Fisher. He pointed, clambering swiftly up the half-hidden stairs that lay behind the tall array of the altar. 'Looks as though there maybe a way out of here.'

At the top of the stairs, a wooden trapdoor covered a splintered exit near the top of the wall. The steps went right up to it, then stopped.

'No use,' muttered Kennett. 'It's bolted from the other side. We'll never get out that way.'

'It's worth a try, anyway,' admitted Fisher. 'Here, let me have a go at it.' He lowered himself slightly, then heaved upwards, throwing the full weight of his athletic body at it. The wood gave a little, and there came a faint splintering from the other side.

'It's yielding,' gasped the other. 'Stand back, I'll try again.' This time, the door fell outwards with a sudden rending crash. Beyond, there was only darkness.

'We made it, Peter. We made it!'

Kennett looked around. There was a

faint glimmering of moonlight, and the ground was less than five feet below them. If they could only squeeze through. Damn it, they had to! He wondered what was happening to the guests and the big hall. Somehow, he had the unshakeable impression that they were very near.

The thought added a desperate urgency to his movements. Within seconds he had thrust his body through the opening, dropping softly to the muddy ground outside. He reached up to help Fisher, smelling the freshness of the cold night air and the rain on the moist earth. Out here, each shadow was stationary, unlike the things that had seemed to move inside the temple.

'You all right, Jim?' he whispered into the velvet darkness.

'Sure. Let's get moving. The sooner we get out of here, the better. Once they find we're missing, there'll be hell to pay.'

They moved silently into the bushes, heading in the direction of the car. There was a half-muted whir of things high above their heads, moving across the silent face the moon. Blurred things, only half-seen, seemed to move with them, closing in on either side.

'Perhaps we'd stand a better chance if we split up,' suggested Fisher. He halted behind the swaying darkness of a bush. 'They might pick up our trail if we stay together, whereas alone, we could make it unseen.'

'All right, if you think that's the best way.' Kennett wasn't too happy about the suggestion, but there was a certain amount of sense in it. And if there was anything after them, it would add confusion if there were two trails.

'I'll go first,' said Fisher. He eased himself up in the darkness, and vanished along a narrow, twisting pathway that curled in and out of the trees. Far ahead, were the lights of the porch, where their car lay.

Kennett waited for a moment, hardly daring to breathe. It was a mad, insane thing they were doing. Why in heaven's name had they come here in the first place? He had the idea that other things were creeping up all around him, watching him with night-seeing eyes, following his every move.

He glanced about him, taking in every detail as his eyes became accustomed to the gloom. Fisher should be well away by now, he decided. There was grass beneath his feet and yellow moonlight above him as he broke cover and raced forward, stumbling and gasping, dodging thorny bushes that reduced his speed.

Someone screamed a little to one side of him. A thin, hideous sound, choked off almost as soon as it had begun. God! that was Fisher. Those fiends had caught him! He forced himself to slow down and turn towards it. Probably there was still something he could do.

Shadowy shapes loomed among the bushes. They were looking for him now, knowing that he couldn't be far away. A tall figure was beating the bushes, trying desperately to locate him. He gasped air down into his aching lungs and lay still, striving madly to merge his body with the dirt. After a while, the shadows and the crackling of feet in the grass faded and went away. Obviously they had given up looking for him now that they had one of the victims. The swaying grass threw a delicate tracery of pattern-shadows on his outstretched hands. With a groan, he pulled himself to his feet, pushing up on his elbows until his arms ached.

Slowly, he made his way back towards the gaunt shadow of the mansion. At least he was free. There might be something he could do. He rounded a bush and saw that the entrance was empty. There was no one there. The tall Creole was gone. Most likely they were all inside, waiting patiently in the huge temple, taking part in the hideous activities, in which Fisher would be the central figure.

Cautiously, he made his way inside. The great hall was deserted. The table had been cleared of the remains of the meal and the candles removed. For a moment, his courage began to fail him. He felt suddenly sick in his stomach.

Somewhere on the other side of that small door, the most horrible service was being enacted. He realised that his nails were cutting into the flesh of his palms. And there was a thin trickle of blood flowing from his lower lip where his teeth had bitten into it. He struggled against something intangible that seemed to be holding him back.

For an instant, it held him immobile, then abruptly, it was gone, and he almost fell forward on his face in the dimness. His fumbling fingers found the heavy drapery, feeling it soft and smooth in his hands. He tugged it silently aside and felt for the handle of the door.

Perhaps it was locked. If that was the case, there was nothing he could do and — He turned it carefully, holding his breath until it hurt. Fear was a living thing inside him and the whole of his body seemed on fire.

The door swung silently open with a sudden motion, almost pitching him into the temple beyond. With an effort, he regained his balance, and leaned back against the hard wood, fighting the madness that was a roaring chaos inside his brain.

The room was full of people with Kestro, small and fat, standing at the huge altar, his back to them. His hands were lifted high above his head, making peculiar motions in the air. On the altar by his side was the thick, black-bound Book of Set, opened in the middle. A silken sash marked the place.

On the opposite side of the altar lay a silver chalice and a blue-shining knife with the blade pointed directly towards the stone slab in the centre. And on the slab —

James Fisher! Kennet almost cried out. So they had caught him. It *had* been his cry he had heard. Jimmy, who never believed in anything evil, who thought the world was such a good place, was now face-to-face with death in its most horrible form.

In the candle-light Kennett managed to catch a glimpse of his face, upturned towards the ceiling, the eyes full of a mute terror that was beyond life. Kestro turned. He was muttering Latin in a dull monotone.

Then he went over to the chalice and handed it to a white-robed Creole, who took it, and stood a little way down from the altar in front of the stone slab on which Fisher lay. Kestro took the knife in his right hand, mumbling words below his breath. His face was afire with a mad, fey light. With a sudden shout, he raised the knife high above his head.

His words, loud and clear in the awful silence that followed, reached Kennett quite easily.

'Now, O Prince of Darkness! Come to take possession of this soul, freely given. Make his mind and spirit one with yours. Take his body so that he may dwell with thee forever.'

'No!' Kennett tried to hurl himself forward. The word stuck in his throat, refusing to come out. His muscles stiffened so that he was unable to move. He seemed to be frozen. There was a numbed sensation chaining him to the spot.

The knife flashed downwards. A sudden chant of fiendish triumph echoed throughout the room. When next Kennett could see properly there was a swirling smoke above the altar, then it thickened, changed, and there was the evil face of the Great Master, leering down at the assembled multitude.

Blackness surged up at him from the ground, from the walls and the ceiling above his head. He passed out with a dull flooding in his brain. Then, with a painful slowness, he came out of it. There was sound again and a shuddering ache that filled every nerve of his body.

He opened his eyes. There was the faint crackle of wood burning and the room seemed vaguely familiar. With an effort that sent blood racing to his brain, he sat upright. Kestro's room. How had he come here?

'Ah, so you've recovered.' God! That accursed voice again. Would it never leave him?

'It was foolish of you to try to escape, of course. But we had one victim for our sacrifice, and that was enough. Your friend Fisher, has joined us for ever now. Don't you agree that he makes a pleasing addition to my little collection?'

'Collection? What the devil are you talking about, Kestro?' Kennett looked about him. And then he saw it! He knew!

Seven little images, where earlier there had been only six! And the seventh!

Something stuck fast in his throat. With an inarticulate cry, he leapt to his feet. There was a mad laughter hanging in the air around him. Wild and insane.

He peered closer to make sure that he hadn't been mistaken. The tiny features were as familiar as his own. God! He had seen them often enough. James Fisher, complete down to the last detail. Even to the clothes he had been wearing when he had been — dead?

No, it was impossible! He must be going mad, raving. He leapt, screaming, for the door. It gave suddenly beneath his fumbling hands. Out through the deserted hall, he ran, shouting and babbling and crashing against tables and chairs.

Then he was outside, running down the silent drive, between the devil-shadows that were the bushes. Behind him, he could dimly hear the wild laughter of Kestro, booming through the house. Words resolved themselves in his ears.

'You've lost Fisher, Kennett. Lost forever. I have his soul now, locked in his tiny image. He won't be coming back, Kennett. Now, he'll stay here forever.'

He turned into the road at the end of the drive. The empty voice faded into silence. The only sound was his own feet splashing through the puddles, and the animal whimpers from his own throat.

3

Shirley's Ghost

My first glimpse of Corvellan as I drove down the steep, winding road towards the coast was far from uplifting. Barely visible through the fog drifting in from the sea, the tiny huddle of cottages along the base of the cliffs looked dismal with their roofs glistening in the drizzling rain. Whenever the fog thinned, the ocean looked sullen and grey, not at all how I imagined it would be.

The fog became thicker by the time I drove along the single narrow street. In spite of the poor visibility, I readily spotted the hotel, it being the only two-storey building in the village. It stood a little way back from the road with a small paved area in front where I parked the car.

Taking my bags inside, I rang the bell on the desk and waited for a few moments before the proprietor arrived, a short, stocky man I guessed to be in his late fifties.

He gave me an inquiring look before his face cleared. 'You'll be Mister Hartley,' he said. 'I expected you earlier but doubtless this terrible weather delayed you.'

After showing me to my room, he paused in the doorway. 'Are you here on holiday, sir? It's just that we get so few visitors to Corvellan, even during the summer.'

'Call it a working holiday,' I told him. 'I'm writing a book on English folklore and superstitions.'

He gave me a sharp look and it was then I remembered that the Cornish people did not regard themselves as being English.

'I don' reckon you'll find many hereabouts willing to talk with strangers. If you're looking for ghosts and the like, I doubt if you'll find much of interest.'

When he had gone, I crossed to the window and stared out into the all-enveloping greyness of the late afternoon.

His last remark had been a little too quick, too vehement, for it to ring true. It was the first inkling I had that there was something about this village that was worth looking into.

That evening, after an excellent dinner, I went through into the bar. There were only two customers, both old men, and clearly locals, sitting in one corner. One of them, the taller of the two, caught my attention at once. He had the weather-beaten features typical of the fishermen along this stretch of coast. His hair was snow white, yet I had the impression that this had happened prematurely, that it was not due merely to age. But it was the expression in his eyes that struck me most forcibly.

I could only describe it as a 'haunted' look. Even without knowing a single thing about him, that expression told me there was something in his past which had laid a heavy burden on him and which would trouble him to his grave.

I turned back to the bartender, a young man barely out of his twenties, with a frank, open face. After ordering a pint, I asked him whether he knew any of the local legends.

He shook his head. 'I'm not from Corvellan,' he told me, leaning his elbows on the bar. 'I'm from Truro, fifteen miles away. If you want to know anything like that, you'll have to ask some of the older folk, though I doubt if they'll tell you much. They're a close-mouthed lot in these parts.'

'I'm quite prepared to pay for any information,' I said, speaking loudly for I knew the two men were listening from their corner.

When neither of them rose to the bait, I took my drink and went over to sit with them.

'Do either of you know of any hauntings in these parts?' I asked directly, eyeing each in turn.

For a moment, neither of them spoke. Then the taller man seated opposite me fixed me with a curious stare and said, 'Do you believe in ghosts yourself, mister?'

'Not really,' I replied honestly. 'Although some of the stories I've heard in the past have made me think.'

'Then why do you waste your time and money asking about them?'

'I suppose it's because there are a lot of people out there who do believe in them and they buy my books.'

The old man shook his head and put down his empty glass on the table.

'It's not wise to mock such things in that way,' he said.

I leaned forward over the table and met his direct stare. 'Then it would seem that you know something. Perhaps you'd care to tell me about it.'

'It's not something I care to talk about.' he replied shortly. 'Especially not to inquisitive strangers.'

With that, he got to his feet and left without another word.

For a moment, I expected his companion to do likewise, but he remained seated.

Seeing his glass was empty, I signalled to the bartender to bring him another. I knew it might be pointless to press him with further questions but I decided to try.

At first he seemed as disinclined to talk as his friend but after another couple of drinks he waxed a little more talkative.

'Old Ben Trevelyan doesn't like to speak of these things,' he said in a low, reedy voice. 'Besides, it all happened a long time ago and he's been a changed man ever since.'

'What exactly did happen?'

'It were more'n twenty years ago. Ben had a boat, the biggest and best vessel in the village. Used to go out fishing every day. Made a good living from it. His boat is still there, moored at the jetty.'

He took a swallow of his beer. 'He married late in life. Pretty young thing she was, much younger than him. Shirley, her name was. Shirley Quaid. Came from Truro, I believe.

'Nobody thought they'd make a go of it, but they did. Leastways for a time. But, after town life, she found Corvellan pretty dull and Ben spent much of his life at sea.'

'So she left him?'

'Reckon it would have been better if she had. But after a time, things got better and she even took to going out with him on his fishing trips. What happened exactly, no one but Ben knows. It were on the night of the big storm, round about this time o' the year. There'd been no hint of anything brewing so Ben took it into his head to go out at night.

'Shirley said she'd go with him. She always was a wild, young thing, head-strong and afraid of nothing. They set off shortly after sundown.'

'Those are dangerous rocks out there just beyond the harbour,' interrupted the bartender. 'And wicked currents.'

'Aye, that's true,' agreed my companion. 'But Ben knew every twist and turn o' currents and every passage through those rocks. But then, around midnight, this storm blew up out o' the south-west without any warning. We all knew Ben had gone out with his wife and most o' the villagers were gathered at the harbour watching for them.

'But a little after two in the morning, when we'd given them up for lost, we sighted the *Shirley* coming in. She'd taken one hell of a battering and there was only Ben on board and he was barely conscious when we got to him. Some reckon he'd been struck on the head by a beam, though how he managed to bring her past those rocks in his condition, no one knows.'

By now, the old man's speech was only just intelligible and he was on the verge of falling asleep.

'I don't think he'll be telling you much more tonight.' The bartender came over and took the old man by the arm. 'Better be on your way home now, Hedley,' he said, helping him to his feet and guiding him unsteadily to the door.

Locking it behind him, he returned to the bar.

'Do you think there's anything in that yarn he just spun me?' I asked.

'I couldn't really say, sir. I've known Hedley Rohan for some time, he's one of our regulars. I doubt if he would have made any of it up.'

Going up to my room half an hour later, I sat by the window, looking out into the night. There was now a full moon riding high in the sky, throwing a net of silver over the water and there, just discernable, I made out the ugly black teeth of the rocks jutting from the water perhaps a quarter of a mile out to sea.

It was easy for me to imagine what it would be like attempting to bring a boat into shelter through the teeth of a raging storm with lightning flashes all around, the thunder rolling overhead, and the angry waves battering the wooden sides.

In spite of my natural scepticism, I had been deeply intrigued by the old man's tale, yet I knew only half of the story. What could have happened out there on that boat more than twenty years earlier during that terrible storm?

Had Shirley Trevelyan been somehow washed overboard and drowned at sea? Or had something far more sinister occurred out there where there were no witnesses?

The next morning, the weather had changed completely. The sun shone from a cloudless blue sky and there was the promise of heat later in the day. After eating a hearty breakfast, I wandered down to the harbour where a long stone jetty thrust out like a tongue into the sea. The tide was now in and there were a number of boats tied up alongside, bobbing up and down in the swell.

A handful of fishermen were seated on the warm stone, repairing their nets. Scanning the length of the jetty, I looked in vain for Ben Trevelyan. Some distance away, however, I spotted the unmistakable figure of my companion of the previous evening.

He glanced up as I approached and I saw his face harden. Sitting down beside him, making sure we were far enough from the others so as not to be overheard, I said: 'Would you like to finish that story you were telling me last night?'

'I don't remember much about last night,' he mumbled. 'If I did say anything, you'd best forget it.'

He made to rise but I caught his arm and pulled him down. After what he had told me, I wasn't going to let him get away as easily as that. 'You were telling me about Ben Trevelyan and how his wife went out with him on the night of the big storm. How only he came back from that trip. So what did happen?'

He stared at me, his wrinkled face twisted into a scowl of indecision and was silent for so long that I thought he had no intention of answering me. Then, lowering his voice to little more than a hoarse, wheezing whisper, he muttered, 'Nobody knows what happened. At the inquest, they said it was accidental death, that she'd been washed overboard in the storm.'

'And you believe that?'

'Doesn't matter what I believe.'

'But you think that Shirley's ghost still comes back to haunt him? Is that what you're hinting at?'

Rohan shook his head slowly. 'There's more to it than that,' he said enigmatically.

'More?'

'Ben was a changed man after that night. He weren't just like a man who'd lost his wife. It were more'n that. He never went out fishing again.'

'That must have been hard for him.'

'It were. That's his craft yonder.' He pointed towards the end of the jetty.

The vessel he indicated was quite large. To my layman's eye, it looked more like a yacht, twin-masted, unlike all of the others, which were engine-powered, it clearly relied on the wind. The wheel was in the bow, open to the elements and, judging by its size, I wondered how a single man could have handled it, even in calm seas.

'A strange craft,' I said.

'Aye. But Ben could make her do anything he wanted.'

'Then why doesn't he sell it if he no longer goes out to sea?'

'Ah, I didn't say he never goes out to sea, just that he no longer does any fishing. He's been known to take her out at night and only when there's a storm brewing. You see, there's only one thing he wants now. To die out there in the middle of a storm, just as she died twenty odd years ago. *But she won't let him die!*'

I swallowed hard, trying to understand the implications of his words. 'What do you mean — she won't let him die?'

'Just that. He wants to join her, out there in the sea. But no matter how hard he tries, she waits for him and always brings that boat back safely to shore.' His mouth parodied a faint grin at my bewildered amazement.

'You're saying that his wife's ghost brings him back to harbour every time he sails out there in the middle of a storm?'

'That's exactly what I'm telling you. I reckon that's her revenge, to make sure he stays alive with that guilt on his soul. There are folk in the village who've seen that boat coming in with the lightning flashing all around it and Shirley standing at the wheel, guiding it through them rocks yonder, hair flying in the wind and the face of a demon.'

'Have you ever seen it?'

'Once,' he muttered after a long pause. 'Only once. And I never want to see it again.'

Somehow, I had the feeling he was telling the truth, that he had seen something. Whether it was a ghost, or simply something conjured up by a vivid imagination, I couldn't be sure.

Before I could question him further, he rose unsteadily to his feet, mumbled something under his breath which sounded like 'I reckon I've said too much', and walked off.

By now, this strange tale had intrigued me to the point where I knew I had to find some answers. A woman who had vanished at sea in mysterious, and possibly sinister, circumstances; stories of a ghost guiding a boat through the storm; and a man filled with guilt who wanted to die but couldn't because of some restless, vengeful spirit which refused to allow him to do so.

I walked down to the end of the jetty to where Trevelyan's boat was moored. The name SHIRLEY was just visible on the bow in large black letters. In places they were almost totally obliterated and it was evident that few repairs had been carried out on the craft for many years. I could see where a couple of deck planks were missing and others split. Much of the metalwork was pitted and rusted.

It certainly didn't appear seaworthy to my untrained eye — and this was the vessel Ben Trevelyan reputedly took out beyond those gaping rocks whenever there was the possibility of a storm. It would be a miracle if she remained afloat by the time the boat was more than a hundred yards from the harbour.

The more I examined it, the more convinced I became that this weird tale was nothing more than superstitious bunkum made up deliberately for my benefit. No doubt Rohan and Trevelyan were secretly laughing between themselves at how easily they had duped this stranger who had come to the village.

Yet back in my room at the hotel, I had the odd feeling that, despite the picturesque tranquility of Corvellan, some dreadful secret from the past still lingered there.

I went to bed early that night, feeling more tired than usual. I could not rid my thoughts of the notion that my probing into this bizarre affair had, in some way, awakened more than just memories in Corvellan. Staring up at the ceiling, I tried to relax. But it proved impossible to sleep. The small room was hot and stuffy and shortly before retiring, I had stepped outside the front door to smoke a cigarette, looking westward to where the sun had just set.

It had been then that I'd noticed the long banks of dark cloud gathered along the horizon and guessed that the hot, sultry day was about to break with thunder. A taut sensation of impending disaster took a firm hold on me.

After an hour of vainly trying to sleep, I got up and went to the window, opening it with difficulty. Outside, the still air was warmer than inside the room. My earlier suspicions were also confirmed when a deep-throated roll of thunder echoed in the distance across the bay.

A wind had got up but it brought no welcome coolness. There was a pale wash of yellow moonlight lying across the cottage roofs but I knew it would soon be extinguished once the storm broke in earnest. Already, ominous black clouds were piling up towards the zenith.

I lit a cigarette and smoked it nervously. The entire village was utterly silent as if holding its breath, waiting for something to happen. I could just make out the white splashes of foam where the sea was beginning to lash against the stone finger of the jetty.

The clock in the tiny church chimed midnight, the final echoes being completely drowned out by a thunderous roar as a vivid bolt of lightning seared across my sight. Jerking back involuntarily, I stood with my hand pressed tightly against the wall, then leaned forward again, oblivious to everything but the sudden, unexpected movement, just visible on the far side of the street.

For a moment, I was sure I had been mistaken. But then I caught a second fragmentary glimpse of the dark figure and I instantly recognized the man who was undoubtedly making his way down to the harbour.

Ben Trevelyan!

But where on earth was he going at that ungodly hour? Then I recalled what Hedley Rohan had told me, something I had not really believed at that time.

Did the stupid fool really intend to go out in that leaking old vessel in the teeth of this storm?

The shape disappeared into the dark

shadows near the end of the street and I found myself tensing nervously as I shifted my gaze to where the length of the jetty was just visible.

I could clearly make out the shape of the SHIRLEY moored at the far end, the masts swaying from side to side as the tide caught her side-on. When the dark, indistinct figure came into view alongside the boat, I was almost expecting it. There was something oddly frightening about the slow, purposeful way the figure moved, stepping awkwardly onto the deck of the pitching vessel.

A sudden lightning glare lit the scene in brilliant monochrome. I saw Trevelyan hoist the sails and then the darkness came rushing in again with only a vivid green haze dancing in front of my straining vision.

When I could see clearly again, the SHIRLEY had been cast off and was away from the harbour, moving slowly towards the narrow gap in the encircling rocks, heading out to sea.

By the time I let myself out of the hotel, the rain was coming down in torrents. With my way lit by vicious lightning flashes, with the thunder roaring like a demon in my ears, with the howling gale tearing at my sodden clothing, I made my way down to the jetty.

There was a solitary figure standing there with his back to me and for a moment, I thought it was Trevelyan. Then I saw it was Rohan. He turned as I came up to him.

'You've seen him? Ben Trevelyan,' he shouted hoarsely. 'He's gone out again, hoping it will be different this time. But he can't escape his fate, no one can.'

I gripped him by the arm. 'Goddamnit, man; I've seen that boat. It's all rotten. He'll never survive.'

'If she wills it, he'll survive. Only to go through with it again and again whenever the storms come.'

Towards the ocean, there was very little visible. Huge waves pounded the beach. Spray stung our eyes as we tried to peer into the pitch blackness.

'He'll not come back yet,' Rohan yelled. 'He's out there somewhere, riding the storm, waiting for her and hoping against hope that the boat founders and he goes down with her. But she won't let him.'

'We must have stood there for almost an hour watching the white horses rolling in from the ocean, hammering against the jetty until it seemed that even the obdurate stone must surely crumble.

Then Rohan's hand gripped my shoulder as he pointed a shaking finger towards the sea.

'*There!*' he shrieked. 'Do you see them?'

Dashing the teeming rain from my eyes, I stared in the direction of the rocks. For several seconds, I saw nothing. Then the entire sky lit up in a glaring sheet of white and I saw everything.

The sails were merely long shreds of cloth, flapping like pennants around the masts. Trevelyan was there on the deck, his hands around the wheel.

And there was another figure beside him.

It was the slim figure of a woman, dressed all in white, her long hair streaming in the wind. Both were struggling violently on the canting deck, hands clamped around the wheel; one striving to turn the vessel onto the rocks and the other, her dress billowing in the gale, struggling to guide it through the narrow gap so that Trevelyan might continue to live with his endless burden of guilt.

'She'll win,' Rohan screamed in my ear. 'She always wins.'

Darkness rushed in to blot out the hideous scene, to erase it temporarily from my sight. I could only stand and try to visualize what was happening just beyond the clawing barrier which waited to tear the bottom out of any hapless vessel unfortunate enough to smash into it.

I could no longer doubt the veracity of the old tales circulating in Corvellan. I knew I was not hallucinating or imagining what I had seen, limned in that lightning glare. Somehow, that boat would drift safely into harbour and Ben Trevelyan would have to live with the memory of cold-blooded murder on his soul.

But then, even above the banshee

shrieking of the gale, we heard a sound that neither of us expected. It was the unmistakable splintering of wood. When the next flash came, it revealed only the raging turmoil of the ocean, funnelling between those two narrow headlands.

Rohan made a curious sign with his left hand, then turned and made his way back along the jetty. I followed him quickly, not wanting to stay another minute in that accursed place.

The next day, I decided to cut short my holiday and leave Corvellan. Something very terrible had happened there two decades earlier and the final act in the drama had been played out the previous night.

In the clear light of day, on that fine, sunny morning, it all seemed like a bad dream. Had I really seen that second figure or had I, in those few seconds when that lightning flash had lit up the scene, merely imagined it? Had it been nothing more than an image conjured up by my overwrought mind, already filled with a chaotic confusion of thoughts brought on by everything I had been told. After packing my things, I went down to the jetty for one last time. By now, the sea was calm and the tide almost out. There was nothing to remind me of what had happened during the night.

Then, just as I was about to retrace my steps, I noticed something in the water. It was nothing more than a plain piece of wood, bobbing gently in the swell. But then an incoming wave suddenly flipped it over and I saw what was on the other side.

It was part of the bow of Trevelyan's boat. But what sent a sudden chill through me and had me hastening from that terrible place, was the name now etched upon it, stark and clear. In deep letters, as if gouged by long, sharp, ragged fingernails — SHIRLEY'S REVENGE!

4

Undersea Quest

In the autumn of 1927, the United States Federal Authorities were approached by Professor Derby of Miskatonic University concerning certain incidents occurring in the seaport town of Innsmouth as told to him by a Robert Olmstead. It had been known for some time that a trade in gold articles existed between Innsmouth and the neighbouring towns of Arkham, Rowley and Ipswich, such items occasionally turning up as far afield as Boston.

However, Olmstead further claimed that illegal immigrants were also present in the town, that a large number of murders had been committed and several people known to have visited Innsmouth had unaccountably disappeared, leaving no clues as to their vanishing.

Acting on this information, two Federal investigators were sent to Innsmouth to look into these claims. When neither man returned, it was decided that an armed raid was to be organized to determine the truth behind the stories of smuggling, murder and the disappearance of a number of individuals.

What happened i8n February 1928 was never released to the public. The testimony of three agents who accompanied this force into Innsmouth, given in three official reports has been kept under lock and key on the orders of the Federal authorities. All subsequent inquiries as to the contents of these reports have been met with the same answer. There never were such documents, the raid was merely to arrest certain individuals for tax evasion, and any suggestions to the contrary are simply pure invention and speculation on the part of the newspapers of that time.

Until now, it has proved impossible to establish whether such reports do indeed exist and, if they do, what is set down in them. The account that follows is based upon photographic copies of the TOP SECRET documents, which have lain in *the archives of the Federal Building for more than seventy years.*

How they come to be in my possession is not only irrelevant but also highly dangerous for certain individuals, including myself. Likewise, the name of the person who obtained them must be protected since, were it to become known, he would certainly face a long period of imprisonment or, like those in Innsmouth, simply vanish off the face of the Earth.

It is true that the events described herein occurred more than half a century ago, that they are so bizarre that few will believe them, and that others will describe them as a deliberate hoax. Yet all were written within two weeks of the raid on Innsmouth by sober, competent agents, all of whom were warned of dire consequences should they speak about the incident to any member of the public.

The decision to publish them now, more than seventy years after the event, has been taken because it is deemed essential that the world should be aware of the lurking horror that may, at any time, emerge and overwhelm mankind.

I

Narrative of Federal agent James P. Curran: February 27, 1928.

My first acquaintance with Innsmouth was in early January 1928. Prior to that I had never heard of the town, nor could I find it marked on any map or listed in any gazetteer. My superiors had instructed me to accompany a colleague, Andrew McAlpine, from the Treasury Department, to Arkham where we were to question a certain Robert Olmstead who wished to give certain information concerning the town.

The drive from Boston to Arkham took the best part of an hour and, with McAlpine at the wheel, I spent the time going through the file that had been given to us. Apparently, Innsmouth was a small seaport town on the north coast of Massachusetts, isolated from, and shunned, by its neighbours. Once a flourishing port, it had decayed and degenerated over the last half century and was now a backward community which kept itself to itself.

Rumours concerning Innsmouth were legion. There were reports of smuggling and the importation of certain natives from some island in the South Seas during the mid-nineteenth century, presumably part of the slave trade. There was certainly a small, but significant, trade in gold items for many of these pieces were on show in Arkham, most of these produced at the Marsh refinery situated on the banks of the Manuxet River.

Reports of murder and unexplained disappearances were also catalogued in the file although whether these were on the scale believed by residents in Arkham and Rowley had not been verified. More recently, during the preceding autumn, two agents from the Treasury Department had been sent to Innsmouth to report on tax evasions and possible contraband passing through Innsmouth. Neither agent had returned and this had brought things to a head as far as the Federal authorities were concerned.

The decision to raid the town had been taken at the highest level and a date set for February. Very little accurate information on conditions inside the town was available. However, an urgent telephone call to the Bureau from Professor Derby of Miskatonic University had resulted in our being ordered to go to the Federal office in Arkham to interview a certain Robert Olmstead who claimed to have recently escaped from Innsmouth and who had important information for us.

Olmstead turned up at the office a little after two that afternoon. He wasn't at all what I had expected. Approximately twenty years old, he gave an address in Cleveland and my first question was why he had travelled such a distance just to visit Innsmouth.

At first, he seemed oddly evasive and kept fidgeting in his chair for a full two minutes before replying. The gist of his reply was that he was attempting to trace his ancestral history back to Arkham and there had discovered that, prior to moving there, his maternal family had originally come from nearby Innsmouth.

'Are you aware that Innsmouth has been under close surveillance by the Federal authorities for some months?' I asked.

He shook his head. 'I know nothing about that,' he declared. 'My only reason for going there was to trace any of my maternal relatives who might still be living in Innsmouth.'

'Then if that was your only reason,' McAlpine put in, 'why did you have to flee for your life as Professor Derby has informed us?'

I could tell at once that he was hiding something from us; that something had happened there which he either didn't want to tell, or was sure we wouldn't believe him.

Then he cleared his throat nervously. 'I spoke with one of the inhabitants, Zadok Allen, who told me things about Innsmouth which the townsfolk don't want the outside world to know. He warned me that if they suspected I'd spoken to him, they'd kill me rather than let any of this information get out.'

'Then I think you'd better tell us what you know,' I said.

'You wouldn't believe a word of it,' he muttered.

'Try us,' McAlpine said.

Moistening his lips, he went on, 'First you have to know there are no religious denominations left in Innsmouth except for one. All of the others were shut down sixty years ago by Obed Marsh who ran the town then. Seemingly, he brought back some pagan religion from some island in the South Pacific, along with a large number of natives. Now they're all members of the Esoteric Order of Dagon.'

'Dagon?' McAlpine inquired.

'Some kind of fish deity. They all believe he lives in some sunken city in the deeps off Devil Reef.'

I nodded. 'We've come across people like this before. Weird cults in the bayou country. But it seems to me that what you're suggesting here might be something more than that.'

'Take my word for it,' he said, and there was no doubting the earnestness in his tone. 'This is far worse than anything you've come up against before. This heathen worship is bad, but there's even worse than that in Innsmouth.'

'Worse?' I prompted, as he hesitated again.

'Much worse. I've seen them and even those I saw aren't as bad as those they've got hidden away in the big houses on Washington, Lafayette and Addams Streets. You can hear about it from the people in Arkham. They call it the Innsmouth look. It comes from the time when those foreigners were brought into the town by Obed Marsh.

'Seems he called up others from the sea off Devil Reef and forced the folk in Innsmouth to mate with them. Call their offspring hybrids, or whatever you like, but they change. Bulging eyes, wide mouths, ears that change into gills. They often swim out to Devil Reef, maybe beyond, and when their time comes, when the change is complete, they leave Innsmouth and go down into the really deep water and remain there for ever in their sunken city they call Y'ha-nthlei.'

I threw my colleague a quick glance at that point. Closing the file in front of me, I said, 'Well, Mister Olmstead, thank you for your information. We'll certainly pass it on to the proper quarter. It will then be up to our superiors as to what action, if any, needs to be taken.'

When he had gone, McAlpine and I sat looking at each other in silence. I had little doubt that something had occurred in Innsmouth to have frightened Olmstead so much that it had sent him running for his life along the abandoned railway line to Rowley.

Once our report had been sent to the Bureau, we heard nothing more until I received orders to report to a Major Fenton, a war veteran, in Boston where I was to place myself under his command.

He turned out to be a short, stocky man in his late forties with dark hair already showing signs of grey.

Taking me aside, he said gruffly, 'I'll expect the fullest cooperation from you. You'll already know something of what's been planned. I also understand you know a little about Innsmouth.'

'Only what I've read in the preliminary file and what I've learned from Robert Olmstead,' I told him.

Without making any further comment, he signalled to one of the officers accompanying him.

A map was spread out on the table and he motioned me forward. 'This is the road from Arkham.' He traced the outline with his forefinger. 'As you see, it enters Innsmouth along Federal Street and continues all the way to the town centre. That's the route we'll take. At the same time, a second force, including the Marine Corps, will enter from the west, while others will go ashore and come in through tunnels which were used for smuggling in the old days.'

'And if some of the inhabitants try to escape by boat?' I asked.

He gave a grim smile. 'We've taken that possibility into account. Three ships will be patrolling the shoreline. They'll take care of anyone attempting to get away by boat.'

Leaning forward, he stabbed a finger at the map. 'One other thing. There may be no truth in this but we do know there's been a lot of activity here, near Devil Reef. For more than a century, contraband has been landed on this reef. It's a dangerous place for vessels but apparently the old sea captains brought natives and other illegal goods there before ferrying them ashore. More importantly as far as we're concerned, there's a two-thousand-foot drop there down to the ocean floor.'

He paused there as if for dramatic effect. Personally, I couldn't see what he was getting at.

'I don't believe half of this myself,' he continued, almost apologetically, 'but from little bits of information we've gathered from a couple of Federal agents who did return from Innsmouth, there's talk in that town of some sunken remains on the seabed in that region.'

'What sort of remains?' asked one of the officers.

Fenton looked across at me. 'You've read the file which was given you some weeks ago. You'll know that every Christian religion has been outlawed in Innsmouth. Everybody there belongs to this weird cult, the Esoteric Order of Dagon. They actually worship this god and believe a sub-sunken city lies at the bottom of the sea, just off the reef, one they call Y'ha-nthlei, where this Dagon lives.'

'Surely you don't believe that, sir,' said the officer.

'I only believe that I can see, Lieutenant. Nevertheless, someone in the government seemed to take it all seriously. A submarine has been ordered to dive down towards the sea bottom and take a look. If there is anything there, they have enough torpedoes on board to blast it to hell and back.'

★ ★ ★

Two days later, I was in a convoy of ten Army trucks approaching the outskirts of Innsmouth. It was now dark and the truck moved without any lights showing. Each of us had received specific orders before we set out. We would stop at the end of Federal Street and from there proceed to the building which housed the

Esoteric Order of Dagon where half of our force would then move off to occupy the Marsh mansion on Washington Street.

Reaching the end of Federal Street, we disembarked. A few dim streetlights shone along its length but nothing showed in any of the once-grand Colonial buildings as we passed, moving from one shadowed doorway to the next. Within five minutes we were within sight of our objective. The building stood facing an open space covered in rough grass. It boasted several massive pillars with the name still visible above the pediment. Its original use as the Masonic Temple still showed where the set-square and pair of compasses of that Order, although partially obliterated by time, were still visible.

Sending twenty men to watch the rear, Major Fenton led the rest of us towards the front door. Not bothering to check whether or not it was locked, he gave the order to smash it down. The rusted hinges yielded readily and, switching on our torches, we rushed inside. A sharp, fishy stench met us, catching horribly at the back of my throat.

In the torchlight we saw that the large lower room was empty apart from a long table flanked by two high-backed chairs.

Then, without warning, a door at the far end of the room suddenly burst open and a horde of dark figures poured into the room. For a moment, I stood absolutely still, abruptly shocked by what the wavering torchlight revealed. I had expected the citizens of this town to offer some resistance to our invasion, but this was something neither I, nor any of the others, had been prepared for.

Only their apparel was normal. They moved forward with a hideous hopping, slithering gait and there was something bordering on the ichthyic, or batrachian, about their leering features. Huge, bulging eyes glared unwinkingly at us from beneath sloping foreheads. Their skin, what little we could see of it, appeared scaled and the wide mouths reminded me of frogs. I think we had all anticipated finding some signs of degeneracy among these folk, but nothing like this.

How such monstrosities had come into being, I was unable to guess. Certainly, the tales of mixed breeding with some other race had some basis in fact.

Uttering guttural croaking sounds, utterly unlike human speech, they threw themselves upon us. Several were clubbed with rifle butts as they attempted to force us back towards the door. Five minutes later, it was all over. Six of them had been killed and the rest were securely tied up. We had lost two men, their faces and chests ripped to shreds by webbed, taloned hands.

Leaving three men to watch the captives, the rest of us followed Major Fenton through the far door. Here there was a flight of stone steps leading down below street level with a faint light just visible at the bottom. The sight which confronted us there was one which shocked all of the warmth from my limbs.

The room was large, even bigger than the one above, decked out in tattered tapestries, all depicting some repellant forms of marine life; giant, octopoid creatures, malformed denizens of the deep and, worst of all, creatures which had the shape of men but with webbed hands and feet and features not dissimilar to those creatures we had just encountered!

The light came from several burning brands set in metal brackets around the walls and by their light we made out the huge altar at the far end, flanked by two massive statues. One was clearly male, the other female — but beyond that they bore no resemblance to anything I had ever seen before.

'What in the name of all that's holy is this place?' Fenton muttered hoarsely, speaking to no one in particular.

Somehow, I forced myself to speak. 'I reckon it's obvious, Major. This is their temple where they worship this heathen god — Dagon. God alone knows what rites they hold down here.'

Fenton's face twisted into a scowl. 'Put a light to it,' he ordered tersely. 'I've seen enough.'

By the time we left the building the flames had taken a firm hold. Through the billowing smoke, we emerged into the street. Already, the sound of rifle fire was coming from several positions around the town centre. Since our orders had been to fire on these people only as a last resort, it was clear that other units had run into serious trouble.

Fifteen minutes later, after fighting our way through a group of yelling figures who attempted to block our path, we linked up with the force which had been sent to raid the Marsh house on Washington Street. They, too, had captured several of the hideously disfigured hybrids. Three of their men had been killed and five wounded during the attack.

After collecting a number of the alien artefacts from the house as evidence, we returned to where we had left the trucks, herding the prisoners on board. For the most part they offered little resistance but I noticed that the men ordered to guard them kept their distance. I could guess how they were feeling and doubted if any of them would ever be the same after what we had uncovered in Innsmouth.

II

Testimony of Federal Agent William T. Darnforth: March 2, 1928.

Acting on sealed orders from the Federal Bureau, I proceeded by train to the small town of Rowley, situated some seven miles west of Innsmouth. My orders were to place myself under the command of Lieutenant Corlson of the Marine Corp. I knew very little concerning Innsmouth, only that a number of Federal agents had disappeared when visiting the town and our task was to enter the place under cover of darkness, proceed to the town centre where it was believed that a number of tunnels, used for more than a century for smuggling contraband into Innsmouth, had their exits.

From the Lieutenant I gathered that our attack would be coordinated with that of a further force moving in from the south. Some resistance was expected and we were to maintain radio contact for as long as possible with two other squads who would be entering the tunnels from the beach. Any of the inhabitants who attempted to flee the town through the tunnels would be trapped between ourselves and those men coming in from the sea.

The first part of our task was accomplished without any serious incident. Small groups of the townsfolk made half-hearted attempts to prevent us advancing along Rowley Road and Dock Street but these scattered for cover after a few shots were fired. As we entered Federal Street north of the bridge across the Manuxet, however, we encountered a larger force and here we were forced to take cover before we finally succeeded in driving them off.

The bridge was the first real obstacle we had to tackle. It was evident at once that it had received no repairs for many years and we had no idea how secure were the ties across the gorge. But now we had progressed this far, there was no turning back. Two at a time, we crossed the decaying structure until we were all safely across.

By now, a number of fires had been

started and the conflagration was spreading rapidly inland from the decaying warehouses along the waterfront, lighting up the sky in that direction.

Reaching the town square we dispersed to search for the hidden entrances to some of the tunnels reputed to exist. It was unlikely they would be well concealed since few visitors ever came to Innsmouth and, from what little information we had of the place, those who did were watched closely. It was not long before we stumbled upon one of them, covered with a thin layer of earth and coarse grass.

There was an iron-runged ladder fastened to the circular side. It didn't look particularly secure, testifying to the fact that the tunnel had probably not been in use for several decades. Lowering ourselves down, we used our torches to delineate our surroundings. The tunnel was larger than I had expected, fully ten feet in height and only a little less in width.

Pools of stagnant water lay everywhere, oozing from the muddy ground and running down the slimy walls. Weird echoes came from somewhere in the blackness ahead of us, and not all of them could be put down to sounds of our own making. I struggled desperately to keep my emotions under tight control for there was something about those faint, elusive sounds which set my nerves on edge, lifting the small hairs on the back of my neck.

Then, still some distance ahead, I made out other noises, more distinct, that increased the tension in my mind. Low, throaty mutterings and occasional piping whistles which seemed oddly out of place down there. In addition, there were faint splashing sounds like objects being dropped into water.

Corlson had also picked them out for he gave a hissed order to halt. In the ensuing silence, we could now hear the noises distinctly although it was impossible to pinpoint their position accurately.

Waving an arm, the Lieutenant signalled us to continue. A few moments later, the torchlight showed where the tunnel turned abruptly to the right and, rounding the bend, where the beams from our torches illuminated the area ahead, we all saw the full horror which dwelt within those accursed tunnels which burrowed like gigantic wormholes through the rock!

It was a scene out of nightmare. Lit by a nauseous green radiance which came from countless luminous algae encrusting the rocks, a vast grotto lay spread out before us. Large stalactites hung from the roof, finding their distorted reflection in a vast pool of sluggish water.

But it was not this that sent me staggering back against the Lieutenant. It was the sight of the indescribable creatures that flopped and floundered around the edge of the black water.

Fish-headed monsters, which belonged only in the mad visions of a deranged mind came surging out of that pool as we emerged onto the slippery, treacherous rocks at its edge. Somewhere there had to be an outlet to the sea for commonsense told me such monstrosities had never evolved on the land.

Several of the men with us seemed on the point of running but Corlson shouted a sudden, urgent command and, somehow, succeeded in bringing them back to their senses. Military discipline reasserted itself. My own actions were instinctive. Bringing up my revolver, I fired several shots into the midst of the slithering creatures. Steeling themselves, the marines opened fire as the Lieutenant signalled to them to spread out and take cover.

How many of the hideous ocean dwellers there were it was impossible to estimate but in the face of the withering rifle fire they were forced to retreat, diving back into the water and disappearing beneath the oily surface. When it was all over, we went forward to examine the bodies. Two of them were still alive with only minor wounds and these were trussed up and left with two men to guard them while we moved on.

Apart from the tunnel along which we had come, three more opened out from around the walls. Checking his compass, the Lieutenant pointed to the one on our left.

'That way,' he said decisively. His voice shook a little. 'The others seem to lead deeper into the town.'

Moving cautiously into the tunnel, now fully aware of the danger that lurked beneath Innsmouth, we went forward in single file, our weapons ready for any further attack. Every man among us had been visibly shaken by our recent experience. Normal degeneracy and inbreeding such as was common among small, isolated communities living in the bayou regions and other townships such as Dunwich, we had expected. But these creatures were something completely different. At that moment, some of the odd stories I had heard from one of the few agents to have spent some time in Innsmouth and left to tell the tale, began to assume something approaching the truth.

In places, the tunnel we were following widened out into wider spaces but here we found nothing more abnormal than driftwood and splintered wooden cases which had evidently been left there to rot by bygone smugglers moving contraband into the town from ships lying off Devil Reef.

Everywhere there was a fishy stench. We had first noticed it on entering the grotto but now it grew stronger and more pronounced and I guessed we were nearing the sea. On occasions, we passed other tunnels branching off from that which we were traversing but only darkness and silence lived in them.

Then, almost an hour after we had lowered ourselves into the depths, a sound did reach us from directly ahead. It began as a faint slithering sound, followed by hoarse croaking gutturals, which bore no resemblance to human speech. Corlson uttered a sharp warning and we immediately switched off our torches, pressing ourselves hard against the slimy, moisture-running walls as we struggled to pinpoint the exact location of the sound.

Soon it became obvious that a large party of creatures were moving rapidly in our direction and a moment later, I picked out more normal sounds superimposed upon the obnoxious mutterings; the shouts of men and guessed that part of the force which had landed on the beach were close on the heels of these unnatural abominations.

A couple of minutes later, stabbing

torchlight showed along the walls of the tunnel, highlighting the large group of Deep Ones now almost upon us. In the confined space of the tunnel with a squad of our own men at the rear, we were unable to open fire on the creatures. Using their bayonets and the butts of their rifles, the Marines clubbed most of them as they struggled to break through our lines. Caught between the two forces, they were speedily overcome. The pitched battle lasted for less than ten minutes.

At the end of that time, seventeen prisoners had been taken, the remainder lying dead on the floor of the tunnel. Three of our force had been killed, their throats slashed.

Linking up with the group from the seaward end of the tunnel, we moved back to where we had left the other prisoners with their two guards. Here we came upon a scene of utter carnage.

It was all too clear what had happened. Those creatures which had escaped us by diving into the pool had returned and clearly in overwhelming numbers. The captives were gone but more than a score of the creatures lay dead on the rocks where the guards had cut them down before being overwhelmed. Of the two men, however, there was no sign. Evidently they had been overpowered after their ammunition had run out and had been dragged into the water.

Corlson gave a muttered oath as he surveyed the scene. 'I should have foreseen this might happen,' he gritted. 'God knows, there must be hundreds, if not thousands, of those creatures somewhere out there in the deep water.'

I tried to reassure him. 'You weren't to know this might happen,' I told him. 'None of us were given any warning of the scale of this infestation. They're like rats in the sewers.'

For a moment I thought that, in his anger at what had happened to his men, he was about to give the order to shoot those captives we had. Then he regained his self-control, rigid discipline took over, and he signalled us to make our way back to the surface.

Once in the town square, we paused to take stock of the situation. Large fires were now burning out of control at several sites but the streets radiating from the square seemed oddly deserted. Either the majority of the citizens were now concealed in the deep cellars across town or had somehow succeeded in fleeing Innsmouth.

Sporadic firing could still be heard but for the most part the town seemed deathly quiet. Over towards the sea, the entire waterfront was now a mass of flame, the conflagration spreading rapidly inland as the fire consumed the ancient wooden buildings.

Corlson gave the order to his men to convey the prisoners to the trucks waiting at the north side of Innsmouth.

Once they were gone, he turned to me. 'I reckon you'll have to put in some kind of report to the Federal Bureau, Darnforth.'

Nodding, I said, 'Whatever I put in it, there aren't going to be many who'll believe a single word. I can't believe most of it myself. All of those nightmare creatures living here or coming up out of the sea! It's against all nature.'

'We've got those captives,' the Lieutenant retorted grimly. 'People will have to believe the evidence of their own eyes.' He threw a swift glance to where the last of the men were disappearing along Federal Street. 'But what in the name of God are those — *things*? Where could they possibly have come from? One thing's for sure, they're not normal inhabitants of this town, no matter how much in-breeding there may have been in the past.'

'I guess the only way any of this makes sense is if you believe in the stories that have been legion in this area concerning Innsmouth for nearly a century,' I told him. 'If it wasn't for what I've witnessed tonight, I'd have said they were nothing more than pure myth and superstition. Now I know different.'

Corlson took out a pack of cigarettes, offered one to me, then nodded. 'You seem to know a little more of this whole affair than I do,' he muttered, blowing smoke into the cold, still air. 'Just what are these odd tales?'

I shrugged. 'All I really know is what's

given in the file I got and what little I picked up in the last couple of weeks, talking to folk in Rowley. Seems some sea-captain, Ober Marsh, brought back this pagan religion from some uncharted island in the South Pacific back in the 1840s and, somehow, converted almost the whole town. Most of the creatures in Innsmouth are hybrids as a result of enforced mating with these natives and with those others, the Deep Ones, who supposedly live in some sunken city — Y'ha-nthlei — that lies on the ocean bottom off Devil Reef.'

'So these Deep Ones also interbred with the town's inhabitants?' Corlson sounded incredulous.

'So they reckon. And they all worship this sea deity — Dagon.'

'God Almighty. This is far worse than anything we've come across before.' He rubbed the back of his hand across his forehead. In spite of the chill, he was sweating. 'So what do you figure the government will do with these prisoners?'

'Keep them all locked up somewhere is my guess. Somehow, I doubt if much of this will ever be released to the general public.'

When we pulled out of Innsmouth five hours later, many of the old buildings and all of the wooden warehouses along the waterfront, were still burning. More than three hundred of the citizens had been taken prisoner.

Later, we heard they had been transferred to special, isolated camps where they were to be interrogated and kept under constant observation. No details as to the exact whereabouts of these camps were to be released.

III

Confidential Report of Federal Investigator Walter C. Tarpey: March 5, 1929

Following special orders received on February 12, 1928, I proceeded by train to Boston, Massachusetts, where I was informed that the government had decided to launch an armed raid on a small fishing port named Innsmouth, some distance along the coast from Arkham. Reports of bootlegging and smuggling of illegal immigrants had apparently been received from several quarters and my orders were to join a submarine, which was to patrol the coast of an island known locally as Devil Reef. This mission was to be coordinated with a land raid upon the town and our task was firstly to prevent any inhabitants escaping by sea (this in conjunction with three vessels of the coastguard) and second, to dive into the deep water off Devil Reef and carry out a survey of the ocean bottom in that region.

It was late afternoon when we were piloted out of the harbour and heading out to sea. Conditions inside the submarine were Spartan, and cramped with little room in which to move. We rode on the surface, accompanied by the other three vessels, the convoy heading north within sight of the coast.

Commander Lowrie had seen service during the war, as had several members of the crew. Apart from myself, however, no one on board knew any details of our mission when we set out, Lowrie having been given sealed orders not to be opened until we were at sea.

Once we arrived offshore from Innsmouth, three of the crew were ordered above, one to man the machine-gun and two others to act as lookouts for any of the townsfolk attempting to escape by boat. With Lowrie's permission, I accompanied them, struggling to maintain my balance against the rolling of the vessel. There was an unusually heavy swell between the shore and Devil Reef, the latter an irregular mass of rock about two miles from the distant harbour.

The night was very still but bitterly cold and I was glad of my thick parka. Despite the darkness, the sky was clear and it was just possible to make out a scattering of lights in the town and at least three fires had been started among the shadowy warehouses that stood along the waterfront.

A sudden hoarse shout from one of the lookouts near the conning tower brought me swiftly around. He was pointing urgently, not in the direction of the town, but out to sea. For several moments, I could make out nothing in that direction to account for his actions. Then, dimly, I saw numerous black shapes in the water, heading towards us from Devil Reef.

Somehow, O'Brien managed to turn the unwieldy machine-gun. Not a moment too soon, he opened fire, swinging the weapon expertly from side to side in a wide arc. Several of the shapes disappeared beneath the waves although it was impossible to determine whether they had been hit. Others still came on and, for the first time, I made out something of their outlines. Those I could see were not even remotely human in appearance. More like fish, but with humanoid bodies and legs, they came surging through the water in a relentless, black tide.

'Get down below!' Somehow, I managed to force the numbness of shock from my mouth and get the words out. 'You can't possibly stop them all, even with that weapon.'

The men obeyed me instantly, lowering themselves quickly through the hatch. Closing it swiftly, O'Brien stared at me in the dim light, an incredulous expression on his bluff features.

'What in the name of all that's holy are those things?'

Before I could reply, there came a clamourous hammering on the hull. It sounded as though there were hundreds of them battering against the tough steel.

Moments later, we heard the Commander's voice giving the order to dive. Hanging on grimly to keep my balance, I experienced a sudden chill as we began to descend. With an effort, I made my way forward.

Here, I found Commander Lowrie at the periscope. He turned and listened grimly as I briefly explained what had happened and what we had seen. Strangely, he didn't appear as surprised as I had expected when I described those creatures, which were now attacking the submarine. It was almost as if he had anticipated something of the kind.

'I've read my orders,' he said harshly. 'Clearly there's some truth in the odd tales which have come out of Innsmouth over the years. Some of them speak of hybrid creatures spawned in the town during the last century and others of the Deep Ones, denizens of some city on the sea bottom. Seems they can exist both on land and in the water.'

'Surely that's not possible,' I said.

'I'm just going by what I've been told. Obviously there's something out here that defies commonsense. But until I find out otherwise, I have to accept these stories, no matter how weird they may seem.'

'What are our orders?' I asked. The battering against the hull had now diminished appreciably. 'Most of those creatures seem to have gone now we're going down.'

'We're to remain at a depth of eighty feet and head west, skirting that reef and head into open water. Then we go down as far as we can and, depending on what we find there, I'll have to make a decision regarding firing the torpedoes we have on board.'

'Then you reckon there may be something down there which has to be destroyed?'

'Maybe.' He paused, then added as an

afterthought, 'I've been in the Navy for nearly thirty years and I've seen some strange things in that time, believe me.'

He motioned towards the search periscope, which, unlike the normal one, had a wide angle of vision. 'We have a very powerful searchlight mounted forward on the hull. Hopefully, we'll be able to use this periscope to see something of what's down there.'

'You won't have much latitude,' I remarked.

'No, but in the circumstances, it's the best we can do.'

Levelling off at eighty feet, we edged slowly oceanward, skirting the reef to the south.

'We have a hydrophone operator on board,' Lowrie explained, 'and he's listening out for obstacles since we don't know accurately how far that reef extends below the surface.'

Twenty minutes later, we had safely navigated the southern edge of the reef and were soon in deeper water. Now, the submarine angled more steeply downward and Commander Lowrie remained at the search periscope, using it for the first time underwater in an attempt to pick out anything visible in the beam from the searchlight.

In this manner, we proceeded to within thirty feet of the ocean floor, then assumed a more even keel. Motioning me forward, he indicated I could take a look at the scene outside. At first, even with my eye pressed hard against the lens, I could see very little. The searchlight beam, powerful as it was, scarcely penetrated more than ten feet into the inky black water. Then something suddenly flashed across my field of view. I caught only the barest glimpse of it before it vanished but that had been sufficient to recognize one of those creatures we had spotted on the surface.

It was followed, instants later, by another and this time I almost cried out at the sight. Whatever it was, I doubted if that creature could ever have been human. It seemed octopoid in outline with tentacles rather than two arms, yet the rest of the body was almost like that of a man!

Beside me, I heard the Commander

issue a terse order. The next moment, we began to descend once more and now, through the periscope, I was able to discern the seabed some thirty feet below. It sloped gradually downward but two minutes later a black, almost straight line of utter darkness appeared directly in front of us, stretching away in an unbroken line in both directions.

I recognized immediately what it was; the dark abyss at the edge of the shallows around Devil Reef, a fathomless deep whose depth we did not know.

Sucking in a deep breath, I relinquished the periscope to the commander and heard his muttered exclamation as he, too, saw it.

'How far down is it possible for us to go without cracking the hull?' I asked.

'Certainly not more than three hundred feet,' he replied. 'More than that I wouldn't like to attempt.'

'That's still a good distance above the bottom if the reports about the depth of this area are accurate.'

'I'm well aware of that, Agent Tarpey. There's nothing in my orders about going to the bottom. There are ten torpedoes on board this vessel. Once we reach the designated position, these are to be fired straight down and then we get out of here.'

'How long before we reach that position?' I inquired. The feeling of claustrophobia, which had made itself felt the moment I had come aboard was now beginning to tell on my nerves. A small number of the men also appeared to be similarly affected.

Lowrie checked his watch, holding it close to his eyes in the dim light. 'Another twelve minutes,' he said briefly. He called Lieutenant Commander Westlock and gave him orders for the torpedoes to be made ready for firing.

While this was being done, I returned to the periscope. Not that I expected to see anything even though the vessel was now descending slowly, but at a steeper angle than before, into the inky blackness of the abyss.

Yet there was something.

At first, my vision refused to take it in. A wavering phosphorescence far below us. I knew that certain deep sea creatures emitted a fluorescent glow — but what I saw covered a vast area and would have required a shoal of millions of such creatures to produce such an effect. Furthermore, there seemed to be an odd regularity about the masses of palely glimmering light. Although it seemed impossible, to me they held ineffable suggestions of structures utterly unlike anything I had ever seen. Squinting, I struggled to imbue them with some form of normality.

How high those alien configurations loomed above the distant ocean floor, it was impossible even to guess, for the glowing radiance seemed to come only from the lowermost regions. But even this was sufficient to show the sheer alienness of their overall outlines.

Had they been nothing more than amorphous masses, it would not have offended my sense of perspective to such a degree. But there were vast bulbous appendages and oddly truncated cones, which intermeshed in angles bearing no relation to Euclidean geometry and I felt my eyes twist horribly as I tried vainly to assimilate everything in my field of vision.

But even this outrage of nature was not the worst. Just before I removed my eye from the periscope, I saw something black and monstrous outlined against the flickering light of that vast city far below. To describe it as tentacled or winged would be to ignore completely the quintessential horror of that slowly ascending shape. I had seen pictures of giant squids reputed to haunt the midnight depths of the ocean but this was far larger, far more abnormal, to belong to that class of creature.

Hearing my sharp exclamation, Commander Lowrie thrust me hurriedly to one side and took my position at the periscope. Clasping the handles in a white-knuckled grip, he turned it slowly. Then, without moving his head, he barked, 'Increase the angle of descent. Ready all torpedoes for immediate firing.'

Once his orders had been carried out, he turned an ashen face in my direction. He seemed to have some difficulty in finding the right words. Finally, he muttered, 'What in God's name is that down there?'

'Y'ha-nthlei, perhaps,' I replied. 'I can't think of anything else. God knows how old that place is. And don't ask me what that — *thing* — is. All I know is that it's coming this way and the sooner we get this over with and surface, the better.'

I could not analyze the reasons for my certitude that whatever that monstrous thing was, we were its target and there was not a moment to be lost if we were to extricate ourselves from this horrible predicament. From what little I had seen, I knew that creature was ten, maybe even twenty, times larger than the submarine and if it succeeded in reaching us, it could drag us down into those alien depths with ease.

In front of me, Lowrie stood, tensed and rigid, at the periscope. I knew he was seeing exactly what I had seen and I firmly believe that the mere sight of that incredible horror might have driven a lesser man over the edge. But he did not flinch. His features set into a mass of grim determination, he waited until he judged the torpedoes would find their mark, then gave the order to fire.

From where we stood, there was little to indicate that the torpedoes were on their way. Five minutes passed with complete silence inside the submarine. Then there came a slight, but distinct, shudder as the detonation waves hit us.

When I stepped forward at Lowrie's gesture to take my last look through the periscope, I was trembling all over. At first, my eyes refused to focus properly. Sucking in a deep breath, I forced myself to remain calm. Slowly, everything became clear.

That frightful distortion of nature I had seen only a few minutes earlier was gone although I thought I caught a fragmentary glimpse of something amorphous dwindling into the depths. As for that vast city, the torpedoes had clearly done their work for here and there were irregular patches of blackness like scars on the overall phosphorescence. Nevertheless, large areas still shone with that sickly radiance and it was evident that, although Y'ha-nthlei, like that creature which had risen to attack us, had been badly damaged, they had not been totally destroyed.

By the time we surfaced, there was no sign of the Deep Ones who had earlier swarmed over the hull. To the west, Innsmouth was burning. The shells of those Colonial houses built of stone would remain as smoke-blackened monuments to the night's raid but almost all of the wooden structures would be reduced to ashes by morning.

I must end this report on a warning note. Innsmouth must remain under close surveillance and a continual watch kept on the ocean just beyond Devil Reef. That which is merely injured, may rise again!

5

Innsnouth Bane

I am writing this narrative in the sincere belief that something terrible has come to Innsmouth; something about which it is not wise to speak openly. Many of my neighbors, if they should ever read this account, will undoubtedly assume that any accusations I make against Obed Marsh are based upon jealousy since there is little doubt that he, alone, is prospering while those of us who lost much during the years of depression are still finding it difficult to profit from this strange upturn in fortune which is his alone.

My name is Jedediah Allen. My family left Boston and settled in Innsmouth in 1676, twenty-one years after the town was founded, my grandfather and father being engaged in trade with the Orient, prospering well following the success of the Revolution. The war of 1812, however, brought misfortune to many Innsmouth families. The loss of men and ships was heavy, the Gilman shipping business suffering particularly badly.

Only Obed Marsh seemed to have come out of the depression successfully. His three vessels, the *Sumatra Queen*, *Hetty* and *Columbia* still made regular sailings to the islands of the South Seas. Yet there was, from the very beginning, something odd about these voyages. From the first, he returned with large quantities of gold trinkets, more treasure than anyone in Innsmouth had ever seen.

One rumor had it that this hoard of gold had been discovered by him concealed in some secret cave on Devil Reef, left there by buccaneers more than two centuries earlier; that he covertly ferried it ashore on nights when there was no moon. Yet having seen some of these artifacts for myself, for Obed displayed many of them quite openly, I was more inclined towards the former explanation as to their origin.

Certainly, the objects were beautiful in

their intricate workmanship and design but this was marred by an alienness in their imagery. All of the objects appeared to have an aquatic motif. To my eye, they had disturbing suggestions of fish or frog symbols, totally unlike any of the Spanish trinkets from the West Indies.

There was also something strange about the metal from which they were fashioned which indicated a non-European source.

My attempts to get Obed to divulge any information about them all met with evasiveness. He would neither confirm nor deny any of the rumors.

There was one man, however, who might talk.

Matt Eliot, first mate on the *Sumatra Queen,* was known to frequent the inn on Water Street whenever he was in port and it was from him that I hoped to learn something.

It was two weeks before an opportunity presented itself. Entering the inn just after dark, I spotted Eliot in the far corner, among the shadows, and for once he appeared to be without his usual drinking companions. After purchasing two drinks, I walked over and sat in the chair opposite him. He clearly had had a lot to drink although the hour was still early.

I knew him to be a man of violent temper, readily aroused, one who had to be approached with caution and diplomacy.

Setting the drink down in front of him, I sat back and studied him closely for several moments. I wanted him to be sufficiently drunk to talk, but not too drunk to fall into a stupor. For a time, he gave no indication that he had noticed my presence. Then his hand went out for the glass and he took several swallows, wiping the back of his hand across his mouth.

Leaning forward, he peered closely at me. Then he grinned. 'Jedediah Allen, ain't it?'

I nodded. 'I'd like to talk with you, Matt,' I said. 'About these voyages you go on with Captain Marsh. Where'd he get all that gold? I'd like to buy some of it for myself.'

His eyes opened and closed several times before he replied, 'Reckon you'll have to speak to Obed about the gold. He keeps all of that for himself.'

'But you do know where he gets it.'

'O' course I do. Every man on those ships knows where that gold comes from.' He leaned forward a little further, pushing his face up to mine, and dropping his voice to a hoarse whisper. 'Every trip he makes, Obed sails for Othaheite. Couple o' years ago, we came across an island to the east not shown on any of our charts. The natives there, the Kanakys, worship some kind o' fish-god and they get all the fish and gold they want in exchange for sacrifices to this heathen god. Obed gives 'em beads and baubles for it.'

He took another swallow of his drink. 'There's somethin' else, somethin' — '

He broke off abruptly as if suddenly aware he was on the point of saying something he shouldn't.

'Go on,' I urged. 'This is just between you and me, Matt.'

'There's another island close to that where the Kanakys live. That's where they offer their sacrifices. Obed got me and

194

two others to row him out there one night. God, it was horrible. Not just the ruins that looked as if they'd lain on the bottom of the sea for millions of years, but what we heard and saw while we were there, on the other side of the island. Things comin' up out o' the sea like fish and frogs only they walked on two legs like men, croakin' and whistlin' like demons.'

I saw him shudder at the memory. 'Obed never went back to that accursed island again. I reckon even he was scared by what we saw.'

Finishing my drink, I thanked him for his information and left. As a staunch member of the Baptist Church, I knew that it was my duty to warn others of Marsh's activities. But without proof, it was doubtful if I would be even listened too. Obed was a prominent figure in town and after all, it had long been an established practice for sea captains to exchange goods with the natives of these far-flung islands. Before I could tell anyone, I needed to know a lot more about what Obed was bringing into

Innsmouth apart from gold.

It was then I decided to wait for his return from his latest voyage. I already knew that both the *Betty* and the *Columbia* had sailed some seven months previously, leaving the *Sumatra Queen* tied up at the harbor for repairs.

Over the next few weeks, I made discreet inquiries concerning these ships and finally ascertained they were due off Innsmouth some five weeks later. I had already decided upon the best vantage point to maintain a close watch on any activity without exposing myself to view. Accordingly, on the night in question, I made my way along Water Street to the harbor. The night was dark and starlit with no moon and I let myself into one of the large warehouses lining the waterfront.

Going up to one of the upper storeys, I crouched down by the window from where I had a clear and unrestricted view of the entire harbor. Although dark, there was sufficient starlight for me to readily make out the irregular black outline of Devil Reef perhaps a mile and a half away.

It was almost midnight when I spotted the two ships rounding Kingsport Head. The *Columbia* was in the lead with the *Hetty* about half a mile astern. Twenty minutes later, after following the movements of the two vessels closely, it became apparent that Marsh meant to bring them both into the harbor rather than anchor offshore.

By the time the vessels had docked a further hour had passed. There was much activity on both ships and the tall figure of Captain Marsh was clearly visible. By shifting my position slightly, I was able to watch closely as the cargoes were unloaded onto the quayside. Much of it consisted of large bales, which were carried into the warehouse adjacent to that in which I had concealed myself. There was little talk among the men, much of the work being carried out in complete silence. After a while, the crews vanished along Water Street and only Marsh and one crewman were left on board the *Columbia.*

When they eventually disembarked

they were carrying a large chest between them and it was this, I guessed, that contained more of the gold which Marsh was bringing back from that unnamed island in the South Seas.

I now had ample confirmation as to the source of this gold and had Marsh continued merely with smuggling such trinkets, there was little that could be said against him. Prior to the war, during the privateering days, such activities were commonplace in Innsmouth and were certainly not frowned upon by the townsfolk.

By now, Marsh seemed to have fully accepted this pagan religion of those natives with whom he traded on a regular basis. He began to speak out vociferously against all of the religious communities, urging anyone who would listen to abandon their Christian faith and worship this pagan god, promising them wealth beyond their wildest dreams if they did so.

Had we all listened to the Reverend Joseph Wallingham who entreated his congregation to have nothing to do with those who worshipped pagan gods and worldly goods; had I known then what I was to discover the next time the *Sumatra Queen* returned from that accursed island, all of the ensuing madness might have been averted.

But few heeded the Reverend Wallingham and it was a further year before that fateful night when the *Sumatra Queen* docked. Is it hard to say what gave me the notion that Obed Marsh was smuggling something more than gold into Innsmouth, nor what brought to my mind the recollection of the old tunnels beneath the town, leading from the sea into the very center of Innsmouth.

But remember them I did. For two nights, I concealed myself on top of the cliff overlooking the shore but without any untoward happenings. On the third night, however, a little before midnight, I observed a party of men moving along the beach from the direction of the harbor. It was clear the men believed themselves to be safe from prying eyes for they carried lanterns and as they drew near the entrance to one of the tunnels, almost immediately below my hiding place, I recognized Obed Marsh in the lead with Matt Eliot and five of the crew close behind.

But it was the sight of the others accompanying them that sent a shiver of nameless dread through me so that I almost cried out. Without doubt they were natives brought back from that terrible island and even in the dim light cast by the bobbing lanterns, I could see there was something distinctly inhuman about them.

Their heads were curiously distorted with long, sloping foreheads, outthrust jaws and bulging eyes like those of a frog or fish. Their gait, too, was peculiar as if they were hopping rather than walking.

Trembling and shaking, I lay there and watched as the party entered the tunnel mouth and disappeared. Not until a full half hour had passed was I able to push myself to my feet and stagger back into town.

God alone knew how many of those creatures Marsh had smuggled into Innsmouth under the unsuspecting noses of the population, concealing them somewhere in his mansion on Washington Street.

At the time, I could tell no one. Marsh had too tight a hold on all who sailed with him for any of them to talk. What dire purpose lay behind this wholesale importation of these natives, I couldn't begin to guess. I knew full well there had to be a reason, but Marsh kept it to himself and none of the creatures were ever seen on the town streets, even after dark.

Over the next two years, whenever he was in town, Marsh continued his tirade against the established churches and when several of the leading churchmen unaccountably disappeared, it became abundantly clear that he intended to become the only force in Innsmouth and those who did not join him also had a tendency to vanish in peculiar circumstances or were driven out of the town.

Then, suddenly and without warning, disaster struck Innsmouth. A terrible epidemic swept through the town, a disease for which there seemed no remedy. Hundreds, including my own wife, died during the outbreak. The few doctors could do nothing to stem the spread of the disease, merely declaring that it was one of foreign origin they had never encountered before. Almost certainly, they maintained, it had been brought into Innsmouth by one of the vessels trading with the Orient.

The dead and dying were everywhere. There was no escape since the Federal authorities, on hearing of it, quarantined the entire town and surrounding region. By the time the contagion had burnt itself out almost half of the population had succumbed.

Now, for the first time, I spoke out of what I had witnessed that night on the cliffs. Other townsfolk then came forward to tell of curious foreigners glimpsed in the fog, particularly along the waterfront at dead of night, some swimming strongly out to sea in the direction of Devil Reef, and many more coming in the other direction.

We knew that something had to be done and a meeting was hurriedly convened to discuss the rapidly deteriorating situation.

There, it was agreed that no other course of action was open to us but to raid the Marsh mansion. Further action would depend upon what we found there. It was essential, of course, that no intimation of this plan should reach Obed for there were now several of the townsfolk who appeared to have thrown in their lot with him.

Two Federal investigators, agents Jensen and Corder, were present at the meeting and although at first reluctant to support this taking of the law into our own hands, they eventually agreed to lead the raid. One group, led by Jensen, would go in at the front while agent Corder would command the second which would enter by the rear.

Arming myself with a pistol, I accompanied the second group. In all, we numbered twenty-two men. None of us knew what to expect as we made our way silently along Lafayette Street towards the rear of the huge building. Once we were in place, we waited for the two blasts on a whistle, which would signal that the other band was ready to move in.

Lights were visible in three of the rear

windows and occasionally a shadow would pass across the curtains. Clearly, the house was occupied but whether the shadows we saw belonged to members of the Marsh family or to servants, it was impossible to tell.

The signal to attack came five minutes later. Running forward, three of the men smashed in the heavy door and moments later, we were inside the house. A long, gloomy corridor led through the house towards the front of the building. Several rooms opened off from it on either side but a quick search revealed only two terrified servants and little out of the ordinary.

Meeting up with the first group we found Obed Marsh seated in a chair before the fire. He had obviously attempted to reach for a weapon when the men had burst in for a pistol lay on the table. Now he sat covered by the revolver in Jensen's hand.

'Did you find anything?' Jensen spoke directly to Corder.

'Nothing in any of the back rooms,' Corder replied. 'But if there is any contraband here, it's likely to be well hidden.'

'You'll find nothing!' Marsh snarled. He half rose to his feet, then sat down again at a gesture from Jensen. 'And you'll all pay for this unwarranted intrusion. I'll make damned sure of that.'

There was something in his threat that sent a shiver through me. I had long known him to be a man who never made idle threats.

While the rest of the men made a thorough search of the other room with five of them climbing the stairs to the upper storeys, I made a slow circuit of the room. Several portraits of the Marsh family members, going back for several generations, hung on the walls but it was not these that made me feel uneasy. There were also other things, lining the mantel-piece above the wide hearth and on top of several long shelves around the walls.

There could be only one place where Marsh could have obtained them. Grotesque statues depicting hideous monstrosities, the likes of which I had never seen before. In particular, I came across a trio of statuettes, each about ten inches in height, which were frightful in the extreme. Apart from the nightmarish contours, which appeared to be hybrids of various sea creatures, the anatomical quintessence of these idols, the grotesque tentacular nature of the limbs and malformed torsos, suggested to me things from some distant pre-human era. The nature of the material from which they were fashioned was also highly peculiar. A pale, nauseous green, striated with minute black lines, it was extremely heavy and none of us could even hazard a guess as to what it was.

A sudden shout from one of the adjoining rooms jerked my attention from them. In a loose bunch, we made our way towards the sound, leaving Jensen to keep an eye on Marsh.

In one of the rooms, the men had come across a locked door which, on being broken down, revealed a flight of stone steps, clearly leading to cellars beneath the house. Lighting three of the lanterns we had brought with us, we descended the steps, almost retching on the stench

206

which came up to meet us. It was a sharp, fishy odor, which caught at the backs of our throats, almost suffocating us.

At the bottom, in the pale light from our lanterns, we saw the shocking confirmation of what I had said earlier concerning my nocturnal vigils on the cliffs. There were more than a score of natives crowded into the cellar and one or two of the men cried out as we tried to assimilate what we saw.

Several of us had sailed to many foreign ports during the prosperous trading and privateering days and were fully conversant with the many native races found on different islands of the Pacific. But what we saw in the wavering lantern light was something none of us had ever witnessed!

These were the most repulsive creatures I had ever set eyes on. Apart from some curious deformity of their bodies, their bulging eyes and oddly shaped heads held something of the aquatic physiognomy of fishes and I could swear that some of them had hands and feet which seemed to be webbed!

Sickened by the sight and smell, I

turned away and it was then I noticed the hastily boarded-up doorway in the far wall where the shadows were thickest. Drawing Corder's attention to it, we soon ripped away the boards and shone the light of one of the lanterns into the gaping aperture that lay behind them. There was no doubting what it was; the opening into one of the old smugglers' tunnels leading down towards the sea.

'So that's how he brought them here,' Corder muttered grimly. 'God alone knows how many more of these creatures are in the town, probably concealed in cellars like this.'

Charged the next day with illegally importing unidentified aliens, Obed Marsh and several of his crew, were thrown into jail to await trial and for two days thereafter an uneasy quiet reigned in Innsmouth.

It was not to last, however. For then came the day which was to change Innsmouth forever.

As far as I was concerned, my suspicions were aroused when I noticed several groups of men in the streets adjoining the jail. All of them were either men who had sailed with Marsh in the past or those who had joined him later when he had spoken out against the various religious denominations.

It was clear their intention was to secure Obed's release by force and this seemed confirmed when they began moving in the direction of Main Street. Hurriedly alerting several of my neighbors and telling them to spread the word, we succeeded in gathering more than fifty men armed with muskets, pikes, knives and any other weapons they could lay their hands on.

By the time we reached the jail we found it had already come under attack. Some of the raiders had forced their way inside and the unmistakable sound of shots came from somewhere within the building. Moments later, we were set upon by the yelling mob and I was fighting for my life against men I had known for years who now acted like crazed madmen.

For a time, since we outnumbered them by almost two to one, we succeeded in driving them back from their objective. But as they retreated along Main Street, a great horde of natives burst out of Waite Street, forcing us back towards the bridge over the Manuxet.

In the distance, I could clearly pick out more gunfire coming from all directions but concentrated mainly near the center of the town and along the waterfront and guessed that fighting had broken out in several places. Already, we had suffered a number of casualties, seven men had been killed and almost twice that number wounded.

Luckily, the majority of the natives were unarmed, relying on sheer weight of numbers to overwhelm us. Several were killed within the first few minutes but the rest came on, heedless of their casualties.

It was the bridge that temporarily saved us. On either side, the riverbank as far as the falls, was far too steep and treacherous to be readily scaled and the Manuxet was in full flood after the recent rains, thereby preventing the creatures from crossing the river and assaulting us from the rear.

For almost an hour we managed to hold off the attackers, inflicting terrible carnage among their ranks. When they began to pull back, we believed we had beaten them off and although firing could still be heard around the town center, it was sporadic, and it appeared the situation was slowly being brought under control.

After what several of us had witnessed in the cellar below the Marsh mansion, I think we believed we were prepared for anything. But nothing could have prepared us for what came next.

It was Silas Benson who suddenly called our attention to the river below us. As I have said, the Manuxet was in full flood but now it teemed with black shapes, swimming upstream against the racing current. That they had come from the sea was immediately obvious. Literally hundreds of them came swarming onto the bank and one horrified glance was enough to show that these creatures were even less human than those we had stumbled upon earlier.

Hopping in a manner hideously suggestive of frogs, they clambered up the steep sides with ease. There was no chance of defeating such a multitude and our only hope of survival was to flee, across the bridge, and along Main Street. Another bank of natives, surging out of Dock Street, attempted to halt us and our ammunition was almost spent by the time we broke through them. Four more of our number was killed before we reached the relative safety of my house where we barricaded ourselves in.

By now it was abundantly clear that those monsters from the sea had taken over the whole of the town. Sporadic firing could still be heard in the distance but we all knew that further resistance was futile.

By the morning of the next day, after spending the night confined to the house, we finally pieced together the full story of what had happened. Obed Marsh and those imprisoned with him had been released. Both of the Federal investigators who had accompanied us to the Marsh mansion had been slaughtered. John Lawrence, editor of the *Innsmouth Courier* on Dock Street, who had often spoken out against Marsh, had been dragged into the street and murdered. The presses and printing equipment had been smashed and the offices set on fire.

Thus it was that Obed Marsh now controlled the whole of Innsmouth. His word was law. Within weeks, the old Masonic Temple on Federal Street had been taken over and replaced by the Esoteric Order of Dagon.

Only a handful of the townsfolk were allowed to leave Innsmouth. These were mostly Lithuanians and Poles. Whether Marsh considered that no one outside Innsmouth would believe anything of what they said about the town or whether, not being descendants of the original settlers, he adjudged them to be of no importance, no one knew. After they had gone, those who remained were allowed to join the Esoteric Order of Dagon. There were few who declined.

It was not only the gold which made

people join this new religion Marsh had brought back with him, nor the fact that, by now, most folk were mortally afraid of him. What persuaded the majority to join was that Marsh promised all who joined that, if they took his five oaths and obeyed him implicitly, they would never die.

When I was asked to join, I refused, as did my son. I had read sufficient concerning the rites that had been practiced in nearby Arkham during the witch trials to know that similar inducements had been made then, that all who worshipped Satan would be granted eternal life. At the time, I knew it to be nothing more than myth and superstition, merely an enticement to get people to join in their unholy rites.

Now, however, I know differently. It soon became apparent that Marsh was involved with those deep ones much more deeply than was first thought. In return for their continued aid, he declared that the townspeople must mate with these creatures. He, himself, was forced to take a wife from among them although she was never seen abroad and no one was able to tell who — or what — she was.

All of that happened almost twenty years ago. More and more of the folk, particularly the younger ones, acquired the same look as many of those natives we had found in Marsh's cellar and some, as the years passed, were even worse, being little different from those creatures which had come from the sea to take over the town. Almost all of the Marsh, Gilman, Hogg and Brewster families were affected by this Innsmouth look. Curiously, Ephraim Waite's family remained untainted even though he was one of Marsh's closest acquaintances.

Rumor had it, however, that Waite had once resided in Arkham and had a reputation as a wizard, some even suggesting that he was the same warlock as was present before and during the witch trials there, two centuries earlier. That this was nothing more than idle gossip, spread by those who were more afraid of him than of Obed Marsh, seemed undeniable.

It was now becoming more difficult and dangerous for me to keep watch on

Marsh's activities. Even though the deep ones had returned to the sea shortly after Marsh's release from jail, a score of years before, those who bore the Innsmouth look were in the majority and any of the population untouched by it were kept under close scrutiny.

Only those who belonged to the Order were allowed in the vicinity of the Esoteric Order of Dagon Hall. Nevertheless, on a number of occasions I managed to approach within fifty yards of it under cover of darkness. Even on those nights when there was no service taking place the building was never silent. Strange echoes seemed to come from somewhere deep beneath the foundations; weird sounds like nothing I had heard before.

But things were worse whenever a service was being held. Just to see some of those who attended made me want to turn and run. Scaled things that wore voluminous clothing to conceal the true shapes of what lay beneath, walking upright like men but with a horrible hopping gait that set my teeth on edge. And the chanting which came from within was something born out of nightmare. Harsh gutturals such as could never have been uttered by normal human throats; croaks and piping whistles, more reminiscent of the frogs and whippoorwills in the hills around Arkham than anything remotely approaching human speech.

Dear Lord — that such blasphemies as those could exist in this sane, everyday world! I found myself on the point of believing some of the tales spread abroad in Innsmouth concerning some deep undersea city, millions of years old, lying on the ocean floor just beyond Devil Reef. When I had first heard them from Elijah Winton, I had immediately dismissed them as the ravings of a madman. But hearing those hideous sounds emanating from the Temple of Dagon made me think again.

Something unutterably evil and terrible lay out there where the seabed reputedly fell sheer for more than two thousand feet into the abyssal depths. Whatever it was, from whatever internal regions it had come, it now held Obed Marsh and his followers in its unbreakable grip.

Then, two days ago, I found myself wandering along Water Street alongside the harbor. What insane compulsion led me in that direction I could not guess. I knew I was being kept under close surveillance all of the way; that eyes were marking my every move.

Where the sense of imminent danger came from it was impossible to tell, nor was it any actual sound. Rather it was a disturbing impression of movement in the vicinity of Marsh Street and Fish Street. I could see nothing to substantiate this but the sensation grew more pronounced as I halted at a spot where it was possible to look out over the breakwater to where Devil Reef thrust its sinister outline above the water.

It was several minutes before I realized there was something different about the contours of that black reef. I had seen it hundreds of times in the past; I knew its outlines like the back of my hand. But now it seemed far higher than normal, almost as if the sea level around it had fallen substantially.

And then I recognized the full,

soul-destroying horror of what I was seeing. That great mass of rock was unchanged. What distorted it was something huge and equally black, which was rising from the sea behind it.

Shuddering convulsively, unable to move a single muscle, I could only stand there, my gaze fixed immutably upon that — *thing* — which rose out of the water until it loomed high above Devil Reef. Mercifully, much of its tremendous bulk lay concealed by the rock and the ocean. Had it all been visible I am certain I would have lost what remained of my sanity in that horror-crazed instant.

There was the impression of a mass of writhing tentacles surrounding a vast, bulbous head, of what looked like great wings outspread behind the shoulders, and a mountainous bulk hidden by the reef. It dripped with great strands of obnoxious seaweed. I knew that, even from that distance, it was aware of me with a malevolent intensity. And there was something more — an aura of utter malignancy which vibrated in the air, filling my mind with images of nightmarish horror.

This, then, was the quintessence of all the evil which had come to Innsmouth; the embodiment of the abomination which Captain Obed Marsh had wittingly, or inadvertently, brought to the town in exchange for gold.

I remember little of my nightmare flight along Marsh Street and South Street. My earliest coherent memory is of slamming and bolting my door and standing, shivering violently, in the hallway. I had thought those creatures which now shambled along the streets of Innsmouth were the final symbolism of evil in this town but that monstrosity I had witnessed out in the bay was infinitely worse.

What mad perversity of nature had produced it, where it had originated, and what its terrible purpose might be, I dreaded to think. I knew it could be none other than Dagon, that pagan god these people now worshipped. I also recognized that I now knew too much, that neither Obed Marsh, nor the deep ones which infested the waters around Innsmouth, could ever allow me to leave and tell of what I had witnessed.

There is only one course open to me. I have set down everything in this narrative and I intend to conceal it where only my son, now serving with the North in the war, which has torn our country apart, can find it.

Through my window I can see the dark, misshapen figures now massing outside and it is not difficult to guess at their intentions. Very soon, they will come to break down the door.

I have to be silenced, and possibly sacrificed, so that the Esoteric Order of Dagon may continue to flourish and the worship of Dagon may go on unhindered.

But I shall thwart whatever plans they have for me. My revolver lies in front of me on the table and there is a single bullet still remaining in the chamber!

THE END

We do hope that you have enjoyed reading this large print book.

Did you know that all of our titles are available for purchase?

We publish a wide range of high quality large print books including:
Romances, Mysteries, Classics
General Fiction
Non Fiction and Westerns

Special interest titles available in large print are:
The Little Oxford Dictionary
Music Book, Song Book
Hymn Book, Service Book

Also available from us courtesy of Oxford University Press:
Young Readers' Dictionary
(large print edition)
Young Readers' Thesaurus
(large print edition)

For further information or a free brochure, please contact us at:
Ulverscroft Large Print Books Ltd.,
The Green, Bradgate Road, Anstey,
Leicester, LE7 7FU, England.
Tel: (00 44) **0116 236 4325**
Fax: (00 44) **0116 234 0205**

ECHO OF BARBARA

John Burke

Imprisoned for ten years, Sam Westwood had clung on by remembering his daughter Barbara. Now released, his main desire was to see her. However, Barbara detested her father's memory, and leaving her mother and her brother Roger at home, she had walked out and could not be found. But Roger had his own reason for wanting Barbara back: a wild scheme which, with the addition of Sam's old associates, would prove to have dangerous complications . . .

THE FACELESS ONES

Gerald Verner

An organisation which was so mysterious and vast, its people had been called 'The Faceless Ones'; their file, held by the British Security Service, was labelled 'Group X'. So who are these people — what are their intentions? Magda Vettrilli had found out, but before she could pass on her knowledge, she was shot on the steps of the British Consulate in Tangier. Egerton Scott must discover their identity, and the objective behind 'Group X'. But can he succeed?